Richard Cumberland

The Choleric Man

A Comedy

Richard Cumberland

The Choleric Man
A Comedy

ISBN/EAN: 9783744772785

Printed in Europe, USA, Canada, Australia, Japan

Cover: Foto ©Andreas Hilbeck / pixelio.de

More available books at **www.hansebooks.com**

A COMEDY.

AS IT IS PERFORMED AT THE

THEATRE-ROYAL

IN

DRURY-LANE.

Jam iftaec infipientia eft,
Sic iram in promptu gerere. PLAUTUS.

By RICHARD CUMBERLAND, Efq.

THE SECOND EDITION.

LONDON:

Printed for T. BECKET, the Corner of the Adelphi in the Strand. 1775.

High and Mighty Sir,

THE attention, with which you have been pleafed to diftinguifh this inconfiderable production, makes it a duty with me to lay it at your feet. The applaufes of the Theatre gave me affurance of its fucccefs, but it was your teftimony alone, which could infpire me with any opinion of its merit: Nor is it on this occafion only I am to thank you; in whatever proportion I have been happy enough to attract the regards of the public, in the fame degree I have never failed being honoured with your's.

How I have merited thefe marks of your partiality I am not able to guefs: I can take my confcience to witnefs, I have paid you no facrifice, devoted no time or ftudy to your fervice; nor am a man in any refpect qualified to repay your favors: Give me credit, there-fore, when I tell you, that your liberality oppreffes me. Was I apt to rate my pretenfions highly, and prefume upon the indulgence of the public, I might have fome claim to your favor; but 'till you hear me complain that my reward is not equal to my merit, I pray you let me enjoy my content and my obfcurity.

At the fame time that I would gladly withdraw my-felf from your notice, I have no one in my eye whom I would wifh to recommend to it: It is my defire to put you at your eafe, worn out as you muft needs be with the toils of your employment; and I ferioufly proteft to you, that if your filence will be the confe-quence of mine, I am ready to enter with you into ar-ticles whenever you think fit; convinced that I can never benefit mankind fo much as by procuring you a lafting repofe; nor would you be long to feek for a retreat; there are many market-towns in the country

where

where you may drink your tea in quiet with a reputable set of elderly maidens at a distance from the capital. Above all things I should humbly recommend it to you, to relieve yourself from your labours in the dramatic walk: Consider, Sir, the campaign is now opening; I understand it will be an active one; new competitors will be pressing forward in the field of fame; I could wish you to keep out of their way; enervated as you are by past excesses, you will be ill able to struggle with these young and maiden spirits; but if you must engage, let it, I pray you, be with some of your intimates, if you find any on the ground; and do not pursue those ministerial politics, hitherto adopted by you, of bestowing all your favours on your opposers, and letting your friends go without their reward.

Whilst I am consulting your future repose, do not think I am unmindful of your past renown: It is to you alone, *Most mighty Sir*, we owe the great encrease of *news-papers* (not to mention *magazines, reviews,* &c.) in this metropolis. In former times, the world was contented with a stale recital of *foreign and domestic occurrences,* which never came to pass, and a lame account of *casualties,* where no mischief was ever done; now the reader is convey'd under your auspices to the foot of the throne; you have the key that admits him into the cabinets of all the princes in Europe; nay, you can carry him a dance thro' the air, as familiarly as the lame devil did the scholar of Salamanca, and uncover the roofs of our closets and chambers to his view: The world is not only supplied with a faithful history of the times in our public prints, but every private family, thro' your means, may meet its own secret *Atalantis*. These are advantages, which some people of confined notions have not clearly understood, and have rashly proceeded to oppose the tyranny of the law against the freedom of the press; pains and penalties have been inflicted, mulcts and imprisonments have been put in force against the conductors of your undertaking; but, thanks to our excellent constitution, you still enjoy your full liberty, though many of your partisans are abridg'd of theirs.

The

The perfonal, political and literary characters of men are the three great branches of your ftudy; eminent have been your refearches in each; but it is not within the compafs of this dedication to follow you thro' any but the latter, and that in the dramatic divifion only: And here I obferve your ordinary practice hath been as follows:

When any play, like this now fubmitted to the public, meets a favourable reception on its firft appearance, the very next morning by break of day out comes your manifefto; unravels the whole plot and contrivance of the drama, diffects the characters, detects the plagiarifms, and kindly tells the town what it is to expect; and all this is the dark operation of one midnight hour, while the poor romantic author lies wrapt perhaps in golden dreams of happinefs and fuccefs: The confequence of this manifefto is, the clearing up of many miftakes which the public would elfe be apt to make: They who have been pleas'd, being told they ought not to have been pleas'd, go no more and avoid an error in judgement; they who would have gone, ftay at home and fave their money; the performers, whom fuccefs might have made giddy, are now prevented from over-acting their feveral parts, and feafonably kept down; the author, whom the plaudits of a theatre might have intoxicated to that phrenzy of fenfibility, in which we are told that * *Philippides the comic poet* expired, is kept in due regimen, and under no danger of lofing the moderate fhare of fenfes you allow him: Thus you ftand, like the admonifhing flave in the triumph, to remind the conqueror that *he is a man*; if therefore the fhouts of the people are loud, you hallow in his ear, fo as to be heard above the cry; if they are moderate, you whifper; but where the people are filent, the admonition is unneceffary; and whenever your own friends mount the carr, your delicacy in their inftance is confpicuous, by the profound taciturnity you obferve.

. * *Philippides quoque Comædiarum poeta haud ignobilis, quum in certamine poetarum, præter fpem viciffet, et lætiffimè gauderet, inter illud gaudium repente mortuus eft.* AULUS GELLIUS iii. xv. .

In

In the inftance of the prefent imperfect performance (thus laid at your feet) I have had opportunity to experience your concern for me in a peculiar manner: Ill-health, and other melancholy attentions, which I need not explain to you, kept me at a diftance from the fcene of its decifion; on this occafion you redoubled your admonitions, apprehenfive, no doubt, that I fhould give way to the flattering report of my friends, and fearful that I fhould yield to that weaknefs, of which the mind, when under the vifitation of affliction, is evidently moft fufceptible.

Nor is this the only error I might have fallen into, I muft confefs to you I had vainly flatter'd myfelf with the defign of addreffing this Comedy not to you, *High and Mighty Sir*, but to an amiable, and elegant friend, to a lady whofe criticifms under favour differ as widely from your's, as *Shakefpeare* does from the author of the *Choleric Man*: This lady, Sir, (whofe name I forbear to mention, as it is unknown to you) was called upon in defence of a countryman to enter the lifts, tho' the mildeft of human beings, with the renowned *Voltaire* (I do not difguife his name from you, becaufe I think on certain fubjects, efpecially where Chriftianity is concerned, you have fometimes taken part with him): The fpectators of the combat gave the victory to the lady; the action is recorded in pure Englifh; but if you pleafe to turn to the particulars of the attack, which was on her fide, you will find it conducted upon principles fo oppofite to your own, that you will probably differ in opinion from the reft of mankind and give your palm to her antagonift: You I know would have proceeded according to all the rules' of modern fineffe; fapping, undermining and blowing up; working like a mole out of fight, and over-turning all things in confufion and ruin; fhe, in the fpirit of ancient times, carried on her approaches in open day-light and above ground, combating with fuch weapons only, as *Greece* and *Rome* had put into her hands under the plain guidance and direction of her own wit and judgement. To this *lady*, in pure affection and efteem, I had purpofed to have infcribed this Comedy; but when you told me

it

it was not worthy even of my poor genius, how could I suppofe it a fit tribute to her's ? She will therefore in the fimple phrafe accept the will for the deed; and if fhe fhould chance upon refufal to diffent from the opinion you have given in the cafe, I muft befeech her to diftruft herfelf, and to believe there is one quality, very apt to miflead and be mifled, which fhe poffeffes in a greater degree (if poffible) than either wit or judgement, and that is called (pardon my introducing it into your prefence) *Benevolence*.

How ridiculous fhould I have made myfelf, if, following the falfe lights of popular applaufe, I had prefented this *heterogeneous* piece (as you are pleafed to call it) to one, whofe genius might have merited the original from whence it pretends to be derived; not the 'Squire of Alfatia* I mean, but the *Adelphi of Terence*: With refpect to the above-mentioned *'Squire*, which I underftand is the offspring of Mr. *Shadwell*, if I have ignorantly robb'd him of any part of his patrimony, I hope it will not be imputed to me; for I do ferioufly declare that to my knowledge I never faw him, or ever had any commerce or acquaintance with him, or knew, 'till you informed me, that he had fo refpectable a father : It is to you therefore, *ingenious Sir*, I am indebted for the difcovery that I have loft fight of an original which I pretended to have copied, and copied one which I really never faw.

But I would beg leave humbly to obferve that the plot of *Terence* was never in my contemplation; it requires the genius of Mr. *Mafon* to make the Grecian fimplicity live on our ftage; I dare not attempt it even at your command; but if you wifh to have it tried, go to your *Terence*, you will find it ingenioufly and ably tranflated, and bring his *Brothers* on the theatre; I fear even my illegitimate race, if tried by a jury of Englifh freeholders, will ouft the reprefentative of the heir apparent, nay the very heir himfelf, if he was to come in his own perfon to affert his right.

Athens and *London*, *Moft Mighty Sir*, cannot as I conceive be eafily compared : In your department I am apprifed how much advantage dwells with the latter; in mine we are grievoufly worfted : I have ventured to hint to you in the dull *prologue* I have prefix'd, that there were at leaſt fifty comic poets flouriſhing at one period in *Athens*, and moſt of theſe lived to write more plays than all our fraternity now alive put together; tho' you I believe may think ſome of us have already written more than enough. *Menander, learned Sir*, you well know is ſaid to have written 80, or according to ſome, 180 Comedies, and that they were all tranſlated by *Terence*; but if we take the teſtimony of ¶*Apollodorus*, the number will amount according to his computation to 105, and the ſame authority tells us that out of theſe 105 Comedies, *Menander* carried away but eight prizes, while §*Euripides*, as *Varro* informs us, on the other hand, out of 75 Tragedies was victorious only in five. Theſe inſtances will ſuffice to give us ſome idea of the comparative ſtate of genius in the two places and periods.

Amongſt all theſe plays and all theſe poets, which the Athenian ſtage can boaſt, I ſhould doubt if you could have found half the employment which our ſcanty fraternity at home afford you: Be pleaſed, *learned Sir*, to try your ſkill upon any one of *Ariſtophanes's* comedies; take his ‡*Clouds* for inſtance; if you was literally in the clouds you could not be more to ſeek; and unleſs Dr. *Johnſon*, or Mrs. *Carter* will take you by the hand (and how that ſhould be I don't know) you will never get thro' the fog—Turn over a Fragment of †*Philemon*; what do you think of it? Write a column in the news-papers upon it; is it not as *heterogeneous* a thing as the *Choleric Man?* Caſt your eye over thoſe paſſages of ‖ *Diphilus*; do you ſee no

---

* *Scripſit* (ſc. Menander) *Suidâ teſte 80 Comædias, vel ſecundum alios* 180, *qui etiam a Terentio converſas eſſe omneſq. intercidiſſe aſſerunt.*

¶ *Ex iſtis tamen centum et quinque omnibus, ſolis eum (ſc. Menandrum) octo viciſſe idem Apollodorus eodem in libro ſcripſit.* A. Gill. xvii. iv.

§ *Euripidem quoq; M Varro ait, quum quinque et ſeptuaginta tragædias ſcripſerit in quinque ſolis viciſſe.*

‡ Νιφίλαι.

† *Philemon lived in the time of Alexander the Great; he was a writer of the* New Comedy, *and is ſaid by Suidas to have written ninety plays.*

‖ *Diphilus was alſo a writer of the* New Comedy; *he wrote* 100 *plays, and ſome of theſe it is ſaid were copied by Plautus.*

reſemblance

refemblance to the *'Squire of Alfatia?* It was as well
known to *Diphilus,* as it is to me.

But there remains a word to be faid on fome learned
animadverfions of your's, entitled *An Effay. on the
Theatre,* in which you profefs to draw a *Comparifon
between Laughing* and *Sentimental Comedy*; and in which
you are pleafed evidently to point fome obfervations
at my comedy of the *Fafhionable Lover:* You infinu-
ate that every blockhead can write *Sentimental or pathetic Comedy*; that *Terence* appears to have made the
neareft approaches, tho' without confounding the different provinces; and yet that he is reproached by
Cæfar for wanting the *vis comica*; but *that all the
other comic writers of antiquity* take the walk of ridicule, and cautioufly avoid incroaching on the confines
of tragedy; nay that *Terence* himfelf judicioufly ftops
fhort before he comes to the * *downright* pathetic.

By this fpecimen of your acquaintance with the
comic writers of antiquity, moft learned Sir, I fufpect
that from the great attention you have beftowed upon
the moderns, you have had little to fpare to their pre-
deceffors; for if it is your opinion that *Terence* of all
the ancient comic poets made the *neareft approaches* to
the *pathetic,* I fear you will have an hoft of authorities
to combat? § *Varro* decrees the province of the
Manners to *Titinnius* and *Terence*; but that of the *Pathetic* to *Trabea, Attilius* and *Cæcilius:* You have here
three comic poets of the Roman ftage, all of which,
according to the teftimony of *Varro* the moft learned
of the Romans, *approached* nearer to the *pathetic* than
Terence. But let us hear the opinion of *C. Cæfar* in
this queftion, to whom you refer us, and tell us

---

* *Terence feems to have made the neareft Approaches, yet always
judicioufly ftops fhort before he comes to the* downwright *pathetic; and
yet he is even reproached by Cæfar for wanting the* Vis comica. *All
the other comic writers of antiquity aim only at rendering folly or vice
ridiculous, but never exalt their characters into bufkin'd pomp, or make
what Voltaire humoroufly calls a tradefman's tragedy.* ANONY.

§ To ethos *nulli alii fervare convenit quam Titinnio et Terentio;
Pathe vero Trabea et Attilius et Cæcilius facilè moverant.* (Varr.
de Lat. Sermone.)

that

that he *reproach'd Terence* for being deficient in the
vis comica, and this no doubt becaufe he had fuch
leanings, fuch *approaches to the pathetic:* The lines,
which convey this *reproach* will be found below in
the † note; they appear to me to be expreffive of a
moft tender affection and refpect to the memory of a
favourite author; and I wifh, *illuftrious Sir,* you would
think fo well of them as to convey your *reproaches* in
the like terms; my brethren would not complain, and
I fhould be a great gainer. But let us confider thefe
expreffions of *Cæfar's*; I do not difcover any allufion
to the *pathetic:* He calls him *puri fermonis amator*;
and this indeed accords with § *Cicero's* defcription;
but I am apt to think that neither in this expreffion, nor
in that of *Lenibus Scriptis* any reference is made to
the *pathetic,* and I am ftrengthened in this opinion by
an obfervation of *Tanaquillus Faber* on this very paf-
fage : * *Cæfar thought* (fays the commentator) *that
Terence, in moving the paffions, was inferior to fome
others, which indeed is the cafe ; and Cæfar's opinion is
confirmed by the decree of Varro, the moft learned of the
Romans.* This truly is to the point, if we are to credit the authority above-mentioned; and he proceeds
to fay, ‡ *Thus you fee that nothing is left to Terence but
The Manners : The Pathetic, which requires force and
energy, efpecially in the comic province, is afcribed to
others.* By this reference you fee we have not only
gained an authority for my interpretation of *Cæfar's*
words, but we have found a learned critic, who is

---

† *Tu quoque tu in fummis, O dimidiate Menander,*
Poneris, et merito, puri fermonis amator ;
Lenibus atque utinam fcriptis adjuncta foret Vis
Comica, *ut æquato virtus polleret honore*
Cum Græcis, neque in hac defpectus parte jaceres,
Unum hoc maceror et doleo tibi deeffe, Terenti.
§ *Quidquid comes loquens ac omnia dulcia dicens.*
* *Nempe hoc fentiebat Terentium in movendis* pathefin *inferiorem
quibufdam poetis effe, quod profecto verum eft, et judicium Cæfaris fen-
tentia Varronis, qui Romanorum doctiffimus fuit, confirmatur.*
‡ *Vides* to ethos *Terentio relictum, nil aliud :* To pathos, *quod
vim et impetum poftulat, præfertim in genere comico, aliis concedi.*

hardy,

hardy enough to affert, that the *pathetic* is the very effence of the *vis comica*, or in other words, *requires force and energy, especially* in *the comic province*; the very oppofite doctrine to what you, *moft learned Sir*, have maintained.

So much for *Terence*; as for *all the other Comic Writers of antiquity*, I am at a lofs to know whether you refer to the whole bulk of them in general, meaning all fuch of whofe writings we have any fragments or defcriptions; or whether you mean *all the others*, whofe plays have come down to us entire; or in other words, *all the two*, viz. *Ariftophanes* and *Plautus*—But we will take a fhort examination of the cafe.

If you mean to refer generally to the bulk of Greek and Roman writers of comedy, the queftion is in part anfwer'd by *Varro*, (as above quoted) who declares that *Trabea, Attilius* and *Cæcilius* excelled in *fentimental* or *pathetic* comedy: This will fatisfy us as to the Roman ftage; the Greek theatre, being original, was more various: Comedy took different characters at different periods: * *The Ancient Comedy* was perfonal and licentious, for then the government of *Athens* was democratical; *Ariftophanes, Cratinus, Eupolis, Pherecrates*, and many others rank under this department; they lafh'd the vices of mankind with fingular feverity; the generals, judges, treafurers, the people themfelves, nay the moft illuftrious and moft virtuous citizens were not exempt from their fatire. Their invectives however were frequently refented; *Eupolis* in particular was caft into the fea and drowned, either becaufe he had fatyriz'd the *Baptæ*, in his comedy fo call'd, or at the command of *Alcibiades*, whom he had lampooned. This circumftance and the tranfition of power from the people to the nobles introduced that fpecies of comedy call'd † *The Middle*; of this fort we are told was the *Æoloficon* of *Ariftophanes*, the *Ulyffes* of *Cratinus*, and many others, which contain no perfonal invective, but have for the object of their

---

* *Vetus Comœdia.* † *Media.*

a 2 ridicule

ridicule certain paſſages in, or alluſions to, the ancient
poets, or parodies and travelties upon the eminent
tragedies; thus *Cratinus* in the comedy above-mentioned ridicules the *Odyſſey*, and thus the tranſition was
made from perſon to performance, much to the
advantage of ſociety: Your tranſitions, *learned Sir*,
on the contrary, are often from performance to perſon.
This however is certain that the writers of the *ancient*
or *middle comedy* made few, if any, *approaches* towards
the *pathetic*, and ſo far your aſſertion is well founded.

But in the ‡ *new comedy*, of which *Menander* is at
the head, the caſe is widely different; the Wits of
Athens became exceedingly cautious how they in-
dulged their vein for ſatire, leaſt by any means their
invective might be applied to any of the *Macedonian*
princes, late *Alexander*'s generals, of whoſe power
they ſtood in extream awe. *Comedy* now aſſumed an
aſpect entirely different; the fragments of *Menander*,
Philemon, *Diphilus*, *Poſidippus*, ||*Apollodorus Gelous*, and
others, conſiſt of moral ſententious paſſages, elegant
in their phraſe, but grave, and many of them,
eſpecially thoſe of *Diphilus*, of a religious caſt, as may
be ſeen by refering to them.

Numberleſs quotations might be adduced to prove
this to have been the character and complexion of the
new comedy under *Menander* and his fraternity;
Quintilian ſays of *Menander* that he is *omnibus rebus,
perſonis*, affectubus *accommodatus*. † *Dion Chryſoſtom*
ſpeaking of his ſtile, ſays it is *imitatio omnium morum
et gratiarum*; and if we may credit * *Clemens
Alexandrinus*, many *paſſages* in *Menander* are

---

‡ *Nova---Novæ Comædiæ Menander fuit facilè princeps.*

|| *The Hecyra and Phormio of Terence are ſaid, by Donatus, to be
taken from Apollodorus.*

† *Namȼ, Menandri imitatio omnium morum et gratiarum omnem ſu-
peravit veterum comicorum vehementiam.*

* *Menander novæ comædiæ princeps unanimiter omnium ore procla-
matur, et proinde juſtare ſibi nomine locum vendicare viſus eſt; quo-
niam ipſius ſententiæ pleræȼ, ab Hebræorum vatibus deſumptæ, quaſi
paraphraſes quorundam propheticorum dictorum ſunt. Teſtis eſt Clemens
Alexandrinus, lib. 5, ςȼȼματιων.* Jac. Hertel. præfatio.

copied

copied from the *Hebrew prophets*: And it is re-
markable that fuch was the elegance and urbanity of
the *Athenian comic poets* under this clafs, at leaft fuch
it appear'd to *Cicero*, that he groups them with the
Socratic philofophers. It will appear therefore that
fentiment or the *pathetic* in comedy was not neglected
by the ancients; that *Terence* fo far from having made
the *neareft approaches* to the *pathetic*, was accufed of
being deficient in it, and others for that very reafon
preferr'd before him, that with refpect to *all the other
comic writers of antiquity*; it cannot be afferted that
ridicule was their fole aim; for tho' it may in general
be fo pronounced of the *ancient and middle comedy*,
yet the writers of the *new comedy*, (who are by far the
moft numerous and moft celebrated) come by no
means under that defcription. As to the pofition that
they never exalt their characters into bufkin'd pomp, &c.
the § prologue to the very firft play in *Plautus*,
learned Sir, well fet you right in that particular;
wherein *Mercury* announces not a *tradefman's tragedy*
indeed, but a *tragi-comedy*.

And now, Sir, having addreffed you under your
general title, do not believe that I mean to mark you
out by any particular one: Your correfpondence with
me, you well know, has always been *anonymous*, ex-
cept in the cafe of one unhappy gentleman, and he
has fled his country. As for you, Sir, wherever you
inhabit, and whatever is your fortune, I bear you no
ill-will; my character I will keep out of your reach,
and for my writings I fhall not much differ in opinion
from you about them: If you purfue the fame
ftudies with me, good luck attend you; give your
own works a good word, and be filent about mine; for
if it fhall pleafe the Giver of my life to fpare it, I
hope foon to prefent to my countrymen fomething
more worthy of their approbation, and lefs dependent
upon your's. I am, &c. &c.

The Author.

---

§ *Quid contraxiftis frontem? quia tragædiam*
Dixi futuram hanc? PLAUT. AMPH.

PROLOGUE.

By the AUTHOR of the COMEDY.

Spoken by Mr. SMITH.

IN Athens once, as *claffic ftory runs,*
Thalia *number'd fifty living fons ;*
But *mark the wafte of time's deftructive hand,*
One *bard furvives of all this numerous band ;*
Yet *human genius feem'd as 'twou'd defy*
Time's *utmoft rage by its variety,*
For *'twas no wond'rous harveft, in thofe days,*
From *one rich ftock to reap a hundred plays.*
Ah ! *could we bring but one of thefe to light,*
We'd *give a hundred fuch as this to-night.*
Rome *from her captive took the law fhe gave,*
And *was at once her miftrefs and her flave ;*
Greece *from her fall immortal triumphs drew,*
And *prov'd her tutelar* Minerva *true :*
She, *goddefs-like, confiding in her charms,*
To Mars *refign'd the barren toil of arms,*
Full *well affur'd, when thefe vain toils were paft,*
That *wit muft triumph over ftrength at laft ;*
Then *fmiling faw her* Athens *meet its doom,*
And *crown'd her in the theatres of* Rome ;
Nor *murmur'd* Rome *to fee her* Terence *fhod*
With *the fame fock in which* Menander *trod,*
Nor Lælius *fcorn'd, nor* Scipio *blufh'd to fit,*
And *join their plaudits to* Athenian *wit.*
Micio's *mild virtue and mad* Demea's *rage,*
With *burfts alternate fhook the echoing ftage ;*
And *from thefe models 'tis your poet draws*
His *beft, his only hope of your applaufe.*
A *tale it is to chace that angry fpleen,*
Which *forms the mirth and moral of his fcene ;*
A *tale for noble and ignoble ear,*
Something *for fathers and for fons to hear :*
And *fhould you on your humbler bard beftow,*
That *grace which* Rome *to her's was pleas'd to fhow,*
Advantage *with the modern fairly lies,*
Who, *lefs deferving, gains as great a prize.*

EPILOGUE.

By Mr. GARRICK.

Spoken by Mrs. ABINGTON.

As I'm an Artift, can my skill do better,
Than paint your pictures? for I'm much your debtor:
I'll draw the out-lines—finish at my leisure,
A groupe like you wou'd be a charming treasure!
Here is my pencil, here my sketching book,
Where for this work, I memorandums took;
I will in full, three quarters, and profile,
Take your sweet faces, nay, your thoughts I'll steal;
From my good friends above, their wives and doxies,
Down to Madame, and Monsieur, in the boxes:
Now for it, Sirs!—I beg from top to bottom,
You'll keep your features fix'd 'till I have got 'em.
First for Fine Gentlemen my fancy stretches—
They'll be more like, the slighter are the sketches:
Such unembodied form invention racks;
Pale cheeks, dead eyes, thin bodies, and long backs;
They would be best in shades, or virgin wax.
To make Fine Ladies like, the toil is vain,
Unless I paint 'em o'er and o'er again:
In frost, tho' not a flower, its charms disclofes,
They can, like hot-houses, produce their roses.
At you, Coquettes, my pencil now takes aim!
In love's Change-Alley playing all the game;
I'll paint you ducklings waddling out quite lame.
The Prude's most virtuous spite, I'll next pourtray;
Railing at gaming—loving private play.
Quitting the gay bon-ton, and wou'd be witty,
I come to you, my Patrons, in the city:
I like your honest, open, English looks;
They show too—that you well employ your cooks!
Have at you now—Nay, Mister—pray don't stir,
Hold up your head, your fat becomes you, Sir;
Leer with your eyes—as thus—now smirk—well done!
You're ogling, Sir—a haunch of venison.
Some of you fickle Patriots I shall pass,
Such brittle beings, will be best on glass.   Now

EPILOGUE.

Now Courtiers you--looks meant your thoughts to smother;
Hands fixt on one thing—eyes upon another;
For Politicians, I have no dark tints,
Such clouded brows are fine for wooden prints.
To distant climes if modern Jasons roam,
And bring the Golden Fleece with curses home,
I'll blacken them with Indian ink—but then
My hands, like theirs, will ne'er be clean again.
Though last, not least in love, I come to * you !
And 'tis with rapture, nature's sons I view;
With warmest tints shall glow your jolly faces,
Joy, love, and laughter, there have fix'd their places,
Free from weak nerves, bon-ton, ennui, and foreign graces.
I'll tire you now no more with pencil strictures;
I'll copy these—next week send home your pictures.

* To the Galleries.

Dramatis Personæ.

MEN.

Andrew Nightshade,	—	Mr. KING,
Manlove,	—	Mr. AICKIN,
Stapleton,	—	Mr. PACKER,
Charles Manlove,	—	Mr. REDDISH,
Jack Nightshade,	—	Mr. WESTON,
Dibble,	—	Mr. BADDELEY,
Gregory,	—	Mr. MOODY,
Frampton,	—	Mr. WALDRON,
Frederick,	—	Mr. WRIGHT.

WOMEN.

Mrs. Stapelton,	—	Mrs. HOPKINS,
Lætitia,	—	Mrs. ABINGTON,
Lucy,	—	Miss POPE,

THE

CHOLERIC MAN.

ACT I.

SCENE I. MANLOVE's *Chambers*.

(FRAMPTON *at his desk*; MANLOVE *enters as from his walk*; FRAMPT. *rises and meets him with some papers.*)

FRAMPTON.

YOU have lengthen'd your walk this morning.

MANLOVE.

Very likely: The gardens were pleasant, and I believe I have rather exceeded my usual stint.

FRAMPTON.

By just one turn upon the terrace.

MANLOVE.

You measur'd me, I see: We men of business, Frampton, contract strange habits of regularity.

FRAMPTON.

And bachelors too, Sir.

MANLOVE.

Very true, very true: A wife now and then does put a man a little out of method, I have heard. Is any body waiting?

FRAMPTON.

No body.

MAN-

MANLOVE.

Any cafes?

FRAMPTON.

Several. (*Gives him papers.*

MANLOVE.

Blefs me! was the world of my mind, they would patch up their differences over a bottle, and let the grafs grow in our Inns of court. Let me fee—what have we got here?—(reads)—*A detects B plucking turnips out of his field*, &c.—Here's a fellow for you, he'll go to law with the Crows for picking worms out of his dunghill: Profecute a fellow-creature for a turnip? A turnip be his damages!

FRAMPTON.

And his food too, at leaft till he's a better man.

MANLOVE.

Nicholas Swanfkin, taylor, in Threadneedle Street, would be glad to know how to proceed in a legal way against his wife, in a cafe of cohabitancy——Had you any fee with this cafe?

FRAMPTON.

A light guinea, Sir.

MANLOVE.

'Tis more than a light woman deferves: Give the taylor his guinea again; bid him proceed to his work, and leave a good-for-nothing wife to go on with her's; and hark'ee, Frampton, you feem to want a new coat, fuppofe you let him take your meafure; the fellow, you fee, would fain be cutting out work for the lawyers. Send Mr. Dibble hither. Oh, he is come.

(DIBBLE *enters with papers.* FRAMPTON *retires to his defk.*)

Mr. Dibble, have you got Mifs Fairfax's papers?

DIBBLE.

They are in my hand, Sir.

MANLOVE.

Have you copied my opinion upon the will?

DIBBLE.

DIBBLE.

It is ready for figning.

(Dibble gives him a pen, and Manlove figns a paper.

MANLOVE.

There, Sir. You've compar'd it, no doubt: Put the papers under one enclofure, and carry them to Mifs Fairfax's; make my refpects, and fay I will have the honour of waiting on her this forenoon, and ftating fome particulars in my opinion that may want explaining.

DIBBLE.

I fhall, Sir. *(Goes to the table and puts up the papers.*

MANLOVE.

Are you ready, Frampton? you and I muft ftep to the hall. How we appear to that fpruce gentleman! His father wore a livery; his fifter is waiting-woman to Mifs Fairfax, the very lady he is going to in that monkey habit: Is there no perfuading him to fuit his drefs to his condition? Believe me, Frampton, there is much good fenfe in old diftinctions: When the law lays down its full-bottom'd perriwig, you will find lefs wifdom in bald pates than you are aware of. *(Exeunt.*

DIBBLE. *(Alone.*

What a damn'd queer figure old Frampton makes of himfelf? I muft never fhow him at our Sunday's club, never. The Counfellor's little better: It does well enough for chamber practice, but he cou'dn't walk the hall in that wig: It's nothing now unlefs a good club of hair peeps under the tye: I hope fhortly to fee the day when Weftminfter-hall fhall be able to count cues with the Parade.—*(He fits down. A knocking at the door.)*—Who's at the door? Come in: You expect now I fhould rife and open it: Not I, in faith, do that office for yourfelf, or ftay where you are.—— Ah, Gregory, is it you! what wind blew you hither? what witch brought you at her back?

SCENE

SCENE II.

Enter GREGORY.

GREGORY.

No witch, but an old bone-fetting mare, with a heavy cloak-bag at her crupper, that has play'd a bitter tune upon my ribs. Where's his honour, Mafter Dibble?

DIBBLE.

Out. Give me hold of thy hand, old boy. What's the beft news in your parts? Hav'n't earth'd old Surly-Boots yet?

GREGORY.

Earth'd him! no fuch luck; he's a tough morfel. He's above ground, as my head can teftify.

(Shows his fcull.

DIBBLE.

Why that's action and battery with a vengeance.

GREGORY.

Battery! he knows the ftrength of my fcull, as well as a fand-man knows the back of his afs, and cudgels it as often: But he's hard at hand—When will his honour, Manlove, be at home?

DIBBLE.

Prefently, prefently. What brings your old blade hither?

GREGORY.

The old errand: a little bit of law; a fma'l jig to the tune of John Doe and Richard Roe; that's all.

DIBBLE.

Plaintiff, I bet five to one. But how does my playmate, Jack? how fares it with young Hopeful?

GREGORY.

Gads-my-life; well remember'd! here's a writing for you: 'Tis a mercilefs fcrawl to be fure; he's not at all come on in his running-hand, not at all; no, tho' I talk to him, and talk to him, and tell him what a fine young man his brother Charles is here, Mr. Manlove I muft call him now; for his honour,

I am

I am told, fince his return from travel, has nominated him afrefh after himfelf, hasn't he, Mafter Dibble?

DIBBLE.

Ay, ay; 'twas done laft feffions; he's no longer Charles Nightfhade, but Charles Manlove, Efq. and a brave eftate he's got by the exchange.

GREGORY.

All thefe things I ding into the ears of our young fcape-grace, Jack; but I might as well whiftle the birds from the fky, as talk him out of his tricks; mobbing with the carter-fellows, and fcampering after the maids: All the while too the arch knave contrives to blind the eyes of old Choleric, his father, fitting as demure as a cat, till he is fairly in for his evening's nap, then away goes he, like hey-go-mad, all the parifh over. Well, have you made out his letter?

DIBBLE.

I'll attempt to read it to you.

Dear Pickle,

Old Choleric is fetting off for London, and thinks to leave me in the country, but it won't do: Muft have another brufh with the lads at the Bear: intend to be at brother Charles's on Wednefday at noon, where you'll meet me. Old Trufty carries this, and underftands trap: Mum's the word. Thine,

JOHN NIGHTSHADE.

So you are privy to this trip, Gregory.

GREGORY.

To be fure, Mafter Dibble; we are all of his fide: There is not a fervant wou'd peach, if he was to commit murder amongft 'em.

DIBBLE.

Indeed! But hold, here is more over the leaf. *Gregory fays I was of age laft Lammas, if you know of ever a clean tight wench, that will take me out of old Choleric's clutches, I don't care if I buckle too for life. N. B. She muft have the Spanifh, or the bait won't take.*

So, fo! he's for a wife you fee: Has he ever talk'd to you in this ftrain?

GREGORY.

Now and then, but I always tell him 'tis time to think of marrying when the old badger is in the earth.

DIBBLE.

Pooh! you're to blame: We'll make a man of him; we'll fet him up with a wife. I have a girl in my eye; a friend of my own—provided you will bear a hand in the bufinefs.

GREGORY.

Bear a hand, Maiter Dibble! You are a lawyer and can take care of yourfelf, I'm a poor fervant and have a character to lofe.

DIBBLE.

Well, well; but if I pay you for your character, and your fervice into the bargain; every thing has its price you know.

GREGORY.

To be fure, there's no denying that: But, hark! here comes his honour Manlove.

DIBBLE.

Enough—Where are you lodg'd?

GREGORY.

At Mr. Stapleton's, in New Broad-Street: I'm going thither after I've feen the counfellor.

DIBBLE.

Better and better ftill: I'm going thither too, and will wait for you below in the fquare: we can difcufs my fcheme by the way.　　　　　[*Exit.*

GREGORY.

What a fharp bitten vermin it is! Ah! thefe law-yers have all their wits about 'em.

SCENE III.

MANLOVE *and* GREGORY.

MANLOVE.

What, Gregory! and without thy mafter? Where's my brother Nightfhade? Thou and he are feldom parted, I believe.　　　　　　　　GRE-

GREGORY.

Troth, Sir, I hope heaven will take some confideration of that, and fet off the fins of my youth againft the fufferings of my old age. The 'Squire is at hand.

MANLOVE.

Well, and what bufinefs calls him up to town?

GREGORY.

Pleafe your honour he is fallen out with our parfon.

MANLOVE.

About tythes?

GREGORY.

Lack-a-day! he has been non-fuited upon that fcore over and over—'Tis about game.

MANLOVE.

Game, quotha! if he comes to talk 'to me about hares and partridges, Gregory, I won't hear of it: Such laws, and fuch law-fuits are the difgrace of the country—I won't hear a word upon the fubject.

GREGORY.

It's quite a breach; he has totally left off going to church himfelf, and forbade all his family; nay, what's more, he has broke his back-gammon tables, only becaufe the parfon taught him the game. Mercy o' me, that ever your honour and my old mafter fhou'd be born of the fame mother.

MANLOVE.

Of the fame mother, but very different fathers, Gregory: Doom'd from early youth to a life merely mercantile, his days have been pafs'd between a compting-houfe at Rotterdam, and the cabbin of a Dutch dogger; precious univerfities! One fon, indeed, he allow'd me to refcue from his hands, and to him I have given a public education; the other poor lad has been a bird of his own breeding.

GREGORY.

And a precious bird he is! fuch another lapwing! fkitting here, and fkitting there; fometimes above, fometimes below: No wonder he's fo wild when his

fchooling

fchooling has been under the hedges; but I hear my
old mafter on the ftairs. Good morning to your
honour—I muft budge onwards to Mr. Stapleton's. ·

[*Exit.*

MANLOVE.

Gregory, good morning.

SCENE IV.

Enter NIGHTSHADE.

NIGHTSHADE (*fpeaks as he enters.*)

I tell you, fellow, there's your fare: I'll not give
you a farthing over. A hard fhilling indeed! a hard
coach if you pleafe!—Brother Manlove, your fervant!
This town grows worfe and worfe; no confcience, no
police—If I was not the moft patient man alive,
fuch things would turn my brain—Brother Manlove,
I fay, your fervant.

MANLOVE.

Brother Andrew, you are welcome. You feem'd a
little ruffled, fo I waited for its fubfiding, and now
give me your hand: I am glad to fee you in town,
provided the occafion be agreeable.

NIGHTSHADE.

I think the law has a provifo for every thing:
Your compliment fets off, like the preamble of a
ftatute, and your conclufion limps after like the
claufe at the tail of it. So you keep your old apart-
ments, and as flovenly as ever—Lincoln's-Inn and
the law—fo runs your life. A turn upon the Terrace
after breakfaft, a mutton chop for dinner at the
Rolls, and the evening papers at the Mount, wind up
your day.

MANLOVE.

A narrow fcale, I own; but whether it be that I
was made too fmall for grandeur, or grandeur be too
fmall for happinefs, I never could entertain both
guefts together, fo I took the humbleft of the two, and
left the other for my betters.

·NIGHT-

NIGHTSHADE.

Ay, 'tis too late to alter; 'twou'd be a vain endeavour to correct your temper at thefe years—By the way, brother, your ftair-cafe is the dirtieft I ever fate my foot upon.

MANLOVE.

So long as we have clean dealings within, our cliants will make no complaint. Your's, I warrant, was neater at Rotterdam?

NIGHTSHADE.

Neater! 'tis matter of aftonifhment to me, how you that have a plentiful eftate, can make yourfelf a flave to bufinefs, and drudge away your life in fuch a hole as this!

MANLOVE.

True, Andrew, 'twas unreafonable; but as I have now made over the beft part of my eftate to your fon, fo I think I have anfwered the beft part of your objection.

NIGHTSHADE.

You fhall excufe me, all the world cries out upon your folly; you are apt to be a little hafty, elfe I fhould be free to tell you, you have made yourfelf ridiculous; and what is worfe, Brother Charles, I fpeak to you as a father, you have undone my fon.

MANLOVE.

How fo? have I confin'd him in his education?

NIGHTSHADE.

No, faith; the fcale on which you've finifh'd him is wide enough to take in vice and folly at full fize; his principles won't cramp their growth. At fchool he was grounded in impudence, the Univerfity confirm'd him in ignorance, and the grand tour ftock'd him with infidelity and bad pictures—fuch has been his education.

MANLOVE.

But you, in your wifdom, purfued a different courfe with your younger fon.

C   NIGHT-

NIGHTSHADE.

I bred him as a rational creature fhould be bred, under the rod of difcipline, under the lafh of my own arm; I gave him a fober, frugal, godly training; and mark the difference between us—Your fellow lives here in this great city, in a round of pleafures, in the front of the fafhion, fquandering and revelling: —Mine abides patiently in the country, toiling and travailing; early at his duty, fparing at his meals, patient of fatigue; he hears no mufic as Charles does, purchafes no fine pictures, lolls in no fine chariot, befools himfelf with no fine women; no, thank my ftars, I've refcued one of my boys; Jack at leaft treads in the fteps of his father.

MANLOVE.

I hope he will; better principles I cannot wifh him; but methinks, Andrew, a little more knowledge of the world——

NIGHTSHADE.

Knowledge of the world, Brother Charles! who knows fo much? Belike you never heard then I had made three trips to Shetland, in a herring-bufs, before you was born? have been three times charter'd to Statia for mufcovadoes; twice to Zante for currants, and made one voyage to Bencoolen for pepper.

MANLOVE.

Yes, and that pepper-voyage runs in your blood ftill.

NIGHTSHADE.

So much the better; it will preferve my wits, it will feafon my underftanding from fuch flyblown folly as your's. Zooks! you to talk of knowledge of the world! where fhould you come by it? upon Clapham-Common? upon Banfted-Downs? Did you ever fee the pike of Teneriffe, the rock of Gibraltar, or even the Bifhop and his Clerks? I know 'em all, your charts, and your coafting-pilots; I have been two nights and a day upon a fandbank in the Grecian
                            Iflands;

Iflands; and do you talk to me of knowledge of the world?

MANLOVE.

Let us change the fubject then—you have not told me what brings you out of the country.

NIGHTSHADE.

Becaufe there's no abiding in it ; what with refractory tenants, poaching parfons, enclofing 'fquires, navigation fchemes, and turnpike meetings, there's no keeping peace about me ; no, tho' I've commenc'd fourteen fuits at law, befides bye-battles at quarter-feffions, courts leet, and courts baron, innumerable.

MANLOVE.

Indeed!

NIGHTSHADE.

No fooner do I put my head out of doors, but inftantly fome fellow meets me with a fowling piece on his fhoulder, or a fifhing-rod in his hand, or a greyhound at his horfe's heels, and all to difturb and deftroy my property.

MANLOVE.

I fay property! let your game look after themfelves. Do you call a creature property, that lights upon my lands to-day, upon your's to-morrow, and the next perhaps in Norway? I reprobate all quarrels about guns, and dogs, and game; for my part I am pleas'd to fee an Englifhman with arms, whether he bears 'em for his own amufement, or for my defence.

NIGHTSHADE.

'Tis mighty well! I am a fool to wafte my time with you; I fhall look after my own game, in my own way; you may watch yours, the fparrows here in the garden, or the old duck in the fountain in the fquare; your fcience goes no farther, fo your fervant; if you want me, I fhall be found at Mr. Stapleton's, in New Broad-ftreet.

MAN-

MANLOVE.

Hold, hold, I'm going there; I've bufinefs at Mr.
Stapleton's; my chariot's at the door—I'll carry you:
Who waits? *(Enter Servant)* Here, take this note
to Mr. Manlove.

NIGHTSHADE.

Ay, that's your puppy; my name wasn't good
enough it feems; but pofitively I'll not fee him; if
you bring him to me 'tis all in vain; I pofitively will
not bear him in my pretence.   [*Exit.*

MANLOVE.

That ever fuch a monfter fhould exift, as an unna-
tural father!   [*Exit.*

SCENE V. *An Apartment in Charles Manlove's House.*

Enter C. MANLOVE, *and* FREDERICK *bis Servant.*

C. MANLOVE.

Mr. Manlove dines with me to-day; lay two covers
in the little parlour, and bid the cook be punctual
to his hour.

FREDERICK.

To a minute, Sir. If Mr. Manlove dines here,
dinner will be ferv'd precifely as the clock is ftriking.

C. MANLOVE.

Set out the dumb waiter, and tell the men they
need not attend. *(Frederick goes and fpeaks at the door.)*
Sir, you cannot come in; my mafter is not to be
fpoken with: Where are you pufhing?

C. MANLOVE.

What's the matter, Frederick?

FREDERICK.

A country-like fellow fays he muft be admitted to
fpeak with you in private; he will not be kept out.
(Pulls the door to, and enters.

C. MANLOVE.

And why fhou'd he?

FREDERICK

FREDERICK.

I don't know; I cannot fay I like his looks; I never faw a more fufpicious perfon.

C. MANLOVE.

Well, let him in, however.

FREDERICK *opens the door and* JACK *enters.*

FREDERICK.

He has the true Tyburn marks about him.　*(afide)*

CHARLES.

Brother!

FREDERICK.

Gad fo, I'm wrong; I'll e'en make off.　[*Exit.*

SCENE VI.

CHA. MANLOVE, *and* JACK NIGHTSHADE.

JACK.

Hufh! hufh! don't blow me; fnug's the word; clofe, clofe, and under the wind.

CHARLES.

I proteft I fcarce knew you, Jack; what brings you to town?

JACK.

Six hours, and as bright a gelding as ever was lapt in leather.

CHARLES.

But what's your bufinefs? did your father fend you up?

JACK.

He fend me up! where have you liv'd to afk the queftion? No, he has brought himfelf hither, and I ftole a march after him: A freak; a frolick, that's all. Didlikins! what a flaming houfe you live in! Oh, I give you joy, brother; Uncle Manlove has clapt a new name upon you. Old Surly knows nothing of this trip. I had much ado to get to the fpeech of you: You've a mortal parcel of fine fellows below in your hall. But you are not angry at my coming? You'll not peach, I hope?

CHARLES.

CHARLES.

· Honour forbid ! Thy lot, my dear boy, has been severe enough.

JACK.

Severe ! there's been no fcarcity of that, I warrant you ; there's not a crab-ftock in the neighbourhood, but what my fhoulders have had a tafte of it's fruit. Oh, you've a rare lot, Charles ! a happy rogue ! Look at me—Who wou'd think you and I were whelps of the fame breed ? You are as fleek as my lady's lap-dog ; I am rough as a water-fpaniel ; be-daggled and be-mir'd, as if I had come out of the fens with wild fowl : Why I have brought off as much foil upon my boots only, as wou'd fet up a Norfolk farmer.

CHARLES.

Well, well, Jack, we'll foon get thee into better trim.

JACK.

Then you muft thruft me into a cafe of your own, for I've no more coats than fkins : Father, to be fure, keeps it well dufted ; but methinks I fhou'd be ftrangely glad to fee myfelf a gentleman for one hour or two.

CHARLES.

What can I do for you ? your father you fay is in town ; a difcovery wou'd be fatal : Do you know where he is lodg'd ?

JACK.

Not I truly ; but my amufements lead to places, where I fhou'd be fure not to meet him : Only one night, dear Charles, and I'll be back again in the country ; think what a life mine is ; compare it with your own, and I'm fure you won't grudge me one day's frolick and away.

CHARLES.

I grudge you ! no—I wifh you cou'd enjoy a bro-ther's fhare in all my happinefs, in all my fortune : Submit, however, to the neceffity of your affairs

with

with a good grace; humour the peculiarities of your father, and command me upon all worthy occasions.

JACK.

Why that's hearty, that's friendly now. Give me hold of your hand. Boddikins, I was afraid you wou'd have turn'd your back on me, now you have jump'd into such a fortune, but I see you are as honest a lad as ever: By the way, Father was in a damn'd hue at your changing your name—fierce as a panther; no man dare enter his den. But you say you'll rigg me out for a day; give me a good launch, Charles, and I warrant I'll find a harbour.

CHARLES.

There's my purse, Jack; it contains enough to spend, and some to throw away: Frederick commands the wardrobe; if you find any thing to your mind, take it; if not, convene my taylor, he'll equip you in an instant: Follow your propensities, but take a little discretion to your aid; your nature has not had much pruning, and 'till experience shall have clear'd the path of life, pleasure may be apt to spread some snares in your way that may cost you sorrow to escape from.

JACK.

Humph! in all twenty and five guineas—What was you saying last, brother?

CHARLES.

Only throwing away a little good advice upon you, Jack; that's all.

JACK.

I thank you; I have a pretty considerable stock of that upon my hands already; one good thing at a time. (*Looking at the money.*) How much of this money must you take back again?

CHARLES.

'Tis all at your service; and more if your occasions require it.

JACK.

J A C K.

Are you ferious? Is it poffible? 'Sbud! I don't
know, I can't tell what I fhould do in your cafe, but
I'm afraid I cou'd never have the heart to give you as
much. Drown it! what pity 'tis that old Crufty
hadn't fome of your fpirit. May I fpend it all, and
won't you require an account of it?

C H A R L E S.

Not unlefs you chufe to give it me.

J A C K.

Give me a kifs, give me a kifs, my dear, dear
brother! enjoy your good fortune and welcome. I
perceive a man hasn't half fo much envy in his heart,
when his pocket's full of money. Come; I'll go
change my drefs.   [*Exeunt.*

A C T   II.

S C E N E I.   *Stapleton's Houfe.*

(STAPLETON *enters to his wife and* LÆTITIA, *who
are difcovered at breakfaft.*)

S T A P L E T O N.

A Merchant's wife, and not breakfafted before
ten! fye upon you, Dolly; thefe are new fafhions,
thefe are courtly cuftoms; let us ftick to the city,
and the old city hours. And this idle jade, Lætitia,
loves her pillow better than fhe does her prayers.
Come, come, away with your crockery: Old Andrew
Nightfhade will be with you before you are aware.

Mrs. S T A P L E T O N.

There is another room ready for his reception. I
am afraid my dear hufband will find this old man's
                                        peevifh-

peevifhnefs more than even his good nature can put up with.

STAPLETON.

Why hav'n't you kept my patience then in better exercife? but never fear. Lætitia you are to have a vifit from Counfellor Manlove this morning: Have you perufed the papers he fent you?

LÆTITIA.

I have.

STAPLETON.

And what do they tell you?

LÆTITIA.

What I can truly teftify, that Mr. Stapleton has been the beft of guardians.

STAPLETON.

I fay the beft! half the trading world wou'd call me a very bad one; when you come to fum up the accounts of your education, Huffy, I expect you will file a bill againft me for wafte and embezzlement.

LÆTITIA.

For mifapplication perhaps; the only objectionable part of your accounts will be the fubject of them.

Mrs. STAPLETON.

For fhame, Lætitia Fairfax; you well know you've been the pride and pleafure of our lives.

STAPLETON.

When fhe was my ward, fhe dare not make fo free with herfelf; now fhe is her own miftrefs, fhe muft do as fhe will: My authority is expired.

LÆTITIA.

Rather reviv'd in fo much fuller force, by how much more I'm bound to you by love, than law.

Enter SERVANT.

SERVANT.

Mr. Nightfhade is below, Sir; Counfellor Manlove to wait upon Mifs Fairfax.

LÆTITIA.

Where have you fhewn him?

D   SER-

SERVANT.

He is in the drawing-room.

LÆTITIA.

I'll wait on him directly.   [*Exit Ser.*

STAPLETON.

A word before we part. Mr. Manlove will inform you of certain restrictions you are under, by your good father's will, in the article of marriage: If the subject shou'd lead him, as possibly it may, to name his nephew Charles to you; in truth, my dear Lætitia, I do not know, in all this town, a young man of whom report speaks so advantagiously.

LÆTITIA.

Mr. Manlove's business with me is of a very different sort.

STAPLETON.

Perhaps not; therefore remember what I say.

LÆTITIA.

I never can forget the respect that is due to your opinion.   [*Exit.*

Mrs. STAPLETON.

Have you any reason to think Mr. Manlove means to propose for his nephew?

STAPLETON.

I'll tell you more of that hereafter; we must now welcome old Nightshade with as good a grace as we can: He is an honest man, tho' a humoursome one, and was for many years a very steady correspondent of mine at Rotterdam. We merchants must not overlook our friends, whatever our betters may think fit to do.   [*Exeunt.*

SCENE II.   *Charles Manlove's House.*

JACK NIGHTSHADE *enters, finely apparell'd, in a suit of his brother's, followed by* DIBBLE.

JACK.

Come along, Dibble, come along—Dear, lovely - and delicious lady fortune, who hast put clothes upon

my

my back, and cafh into my pocket! thou know'ft I never flander'd thee, never call'd thee jilt or gypfey, when I've feen thee perch'd upon thy wheel, and feeding fools by handfuls; give me now the reft of thy bleffings, love, pleafure, and good fellowfhip! May the lads I am to meet be frolickfome, and the laffes free! and never let my poor little defencelefs wherry come athwart that old Dutch dogger, my father, till it's fafe in harbour, and all hands afhore.

DIBBLE.

Well faid, 'Squire, where in the name of wonder did you find this rhapfody?

JACK.

Why, did you never fee the picture of fortune, mounted on a wheel with a bandage over her eyes, toffing money to the mob, like a parliament man? Gregory has the print in his pantry, you may buy the whole moral for a penny.

DIBBLE.

I proteft, Jack, you are not only grown a beau in your brother's fine clothes, but a wit into the bargain.

JACK.

Pfhaw! I am merry enough when my belly's full, and father afleep; but what fignifies a poor fellow's being witty, when there's nobody to laugh at his jokes? 'Tis the money in my pocket, Dibble, not the clothes on my back makes me a wit; and when the wine mounts into my noddle, I fhall be wittier ftill.

DIBBLE.

Time will fhew; but hark'ee, 'Squire Jack, before you pafs yourfelf off for a man of fafhion, fhou'dn't you practice the carriage and conceits of one?

JACK.

I fhall be glad to learn.

DIBBLE.

Be ruled by me; I will give you a few leffons fhall fet you up for a fine gentleman in a minute.

Look

Look at me—that's well. Stare me full in the face—Ay, that will do—you've impudence enough for the character, that's a main point gain'd—now walk acrofs the room.

JACK.

Walk! why that's eafy enough I hope.

DIBBLE.

Hold, not fo faft; there you are out—walk trippingly thus, dy'e fee, with a lazy loitering air, not a league at a ftride, with your head playing like the pole of a coach, fo *(mimicking.)* When you enter a room, take no notice of any body in it; make your way ftrait to the chimney, turn your back to the fire, pull away the flaps of your clothes, and difplay your perfon to the ladies who are fitting round it; when their teeth begin to chatter with the cold, throw yourfelf careleffy into a chair, tuck your hands into your muff, and never open your lips for the reft of the afternoon---'twill gain refpect in every houfe you enter.

JACK.

Well, well, Dibble, this is all eafy enough: I fhall be moft at a lofs for the lingo—what wou'd your worfhip have me fay when I'm amongft my betters?

DIBBLE.

Nothing, I tell you.

JACK.

Nothing! how the duce then fhall I fhew my wit?

DIBBLE.

By holding your tongue; never fpeak yourfelf, nor fmile at any thing fpoken by another; referve your wit for your creditors, they'll keep it in exercife; not but what there are other occafions for a man of fafhion to fhew his parts; as for inftance, with a woman of modefty you may be witty at the expence of her blufhes, or with a parfon at the expence of his profeffion; thefe are cheap methods, be at no pains in the account, decency and religion will pay all cofts, and you'll be clear of the courts.

JACK.

JACK.

You need not tell me that; why I've play'd a thousand tricks upon our vicar, and as for modest women as you call 'em, I don't know much of them; but I know my tongue runs fast enough when I'm amongst the maids, I can set the whole kitchen in a roar—But come, let's sally: Now do you mind, Dibble, don't you be calling me 'Squire, and 'Squire Jack, and Jack Nightshade; but let it be Sir, and your honour, and all that.

DIBBLE.

Trust to me for setting you off in those fine clothes—let me see—what shall I say you are?

JACK.

Say I'm a young West Indian just come to my canes.

DIBBLE.

Ay, or a young nobleman just succeeded to your honours—'twill account for your want of education.

JACK.

No, hang it, a better thought strikes me—call me Mr. Manlove.

DIBBLE.

Mr. Manlove! why do you take your brother's name?

JACK.

For the same reason I take his clothes—because it fits me: If I leave him the estate that came with it, why mayn't I change names as well as he?

DIBBLE.

Because he chang'd by act of parliament, and you by act of your own.

JACK.

Act of parliament! egad they'll change people's sexes by-and-by; why they'll turn a wife into a maid by act of parliament as readily as a common into an enclosure.

DIB-

DIBBLE.

Yes, but it generally remains common for the life of the proprietor.

JACK.

Nan!—How muſt I carry my hat, Dibble? thus, under my arm? This damn'd barber has thruſt his black ſkewers thro' my ears.—Look out and tell me if the man has call'd a coach.

DIBBLE.

'Tis waiting, Sir.

JACK.

A plague upon this ſpit! 'tis as heavy as a fowling pouch, and jingles like a pair of dog-couples; an oak-ſtick is worth two of it, Have you caution'd the ſervants about my name?

DIBBLE.

'Tis done, your honour.

JACK.

'Tis done, your honour—your honour is obeyed: Come along, Dibble, let honour go before, and law follow after.

DIBBLE.

Ay, but when law is at your heels, have a care it does not overtake you.   [Exeunt.

SCENE III.

Enter MANLOVE, and CHARLES.

MANLOVE.

Her mother was a Sedley, of a reſpectable family, and an accompliſh'd lady; her father was a trader of fair character and principal in the houſe now conducted with ſuch credit by her guardian Stapleton; her fortune is conſiderable; I mention that to you, as I think any great diſproportion on either ſide in that particular is to be avoided.

CHARLES.

CHARLES.

Equal alliances to be sure are best.

MANLOVE.

And this would be of all most equal, for I verily think you have not a virtue, of which Miss Fairfax does not possess the counterpart: By the way, Charles, you will not like her the worse for being no inconsiderable proficient in your favourite art, painting.

CHARLES.

I have heard her performance very highly commended: Your report makes me ambitious of being known to her; and so, my dear Sir, I promise you, in the words of your favourite poet,

I'll look to like, if looking liking move.

I'll take my heart to counsel, for I know you ask no sacrifice.

MANLOVE.

No, Charles, 'twas to make you free, not to rob you of your freedom, that I gave you a fortune; if I throw your inclination into fetters, 'twill be poor satisfaction that I gilt them over afterwards.

CHARLES.

In that assurance I will proceed in this affair after my own humour; for as I wish to have an opportunity of seeing this fair paintress in her natural colours, I must devise some method of conversing with her at my ease.

MANLOVE.

At your ease? what prevents you?

CHARLES.

The declaration you made to her this morning; I dread the artificial graces which young women are too apt to put on, when they act under observation; so quiet, so chastis'd, so infinitely obliging: We think 'em meek as lambs; marry 'em, and they change to mountain-cats. Such women remind me of decay'd ships newly painted; the outside is inviting; embark, and they conduct you to your grave.

MAN-

MANLOVE.

Well, Charles, if you embark your hopes upon
this venture, I think I may enfure your happinefs,
though the voyage is for life.

CHARLES.

Where can I find a better policy? However, if I
could meet her without her knowing me—in the way
of her art now, can you tell me, is fhe vifited by our
beft mafters?

MANLOVE.

·By all; foreigners as well as natives; there is no
fame without her approbation; not a grace is ftampt
without her fiat.

CHARLES.

Under favour, are not thefe extraordinary accomplifhments to acquire in the family of a trader?

MANLOVE.

Not at all; beware how you apply French ideas
to Englifh merchants: Where nature beftows genius,
education will give accomplifhments; but where the
difpofition is wanting, the blood of a Duchefs cannot make a gentlewoman.

CHARLES.

Was fhe ever out of England?

MANLOVE.

I have been told fhe was near two years in Italy
with a family of diftinction.

CHARLES.

It is enough; I have my cue: I think I fhall fall
upon a method of introducing myfelf to her acquaintance without a difcovery. I can pafs examination in
the art of painting very tolerably.

MANLOVE.

Take your own courfe; I have no right to advife;
I am poor authority in affairs of love. Good after-
noon to you. Nay, Charles, no ceremony; I thought
we had agreed on that. Your fervant.   [*Exit.*

CHARLES.

Your moft obedient—Here, who waits?

Enter

Enter FREDERICK.

Frederick, look out my travelling frock, you know which I mean.

FREDERICK.

The fuit you had made at Lyons.

CHARLES.

No, 'twas at Milan : The green camblet : Bring it to me in the dreſſing-room.   Make haſte.

[*Exeunt ſeverally.*]

SCENE IV.

NIGHTSHADE, *followed by* FRAMPTON.

NIGHTSHADE.

Come along, Mr. What's-your-name : Enter with-out more ceremony I befeech you—An old formal blockhead !

FRAMPTON.

I attend you, Sir, by order of Mr. Manlove, touching a cafe wherein you have confulted him.

NIGHTSHADE.

That's true, that's true ; it is the pigeon-houfe cafe—I gave it him this morning : Is it ufual for you lawyers to be fo nimble with your anfwers ?

FRAMPTON.

It is not unufual with Mr. Manlove.

NIGHTSHADE.

Well, and what thinks he of the cafe?

FRAMPTON.

The cafe is a clear cafe.

NIGHTSHADE.

I am glad to hear it heartily.

FRAMPTON.

In other words, it is a cafe clear to be apprehended : It hath reference to a pigeon-houfe, built and erected in a certain field, commonly known by the name of the Vicar's Homeſtead. *Quære : Standeth not the ſaid pigeon-houſe within the manorial rights of Calves-Town, and in that cafe, may not you, Andrew Night-*

E   *ſhade,*

*shade, Esq. lord of said manor, remove, or cause to be
remov'd, said vicar's pigeon-house.*

NIGHTSHADE.

Pull down, erase, destroy, and level with the
ground; those are my words. Now give me 'the
opinion.

FRAMPTON.

He has given no opinion.

NIGHTSHADE.

No opinion! what the plague is this your errand?
Am I to be made a fool of?

FRAMPTON.

To his clients Mr. Manlove gives opinions, to his
friends advice. He wishes you to let the pigeon-
house stand where it does.

NIGHTSHADE.

A fig for what he wishes.

FRAMPTON.

However, if you're so determin'd, he does not
deny but you may pull it down.

NIGHTSHADE.

Why that's enough. Then down it goes: I'll sow
the land with salt.

FRAMPTON.

Nevertheless, he wills me to tell you, that this
must be done *tuo periculo*, as the saying is; for if your
conscience does not prevent you from pulling it down,
the law will make you build it up again.

NIGHTSHADE.

The law has made a fool of you, methinks: Why,
what the deuce do you blow hot and cold in the same
breath? Is this the way you treat your clients? Am
I to be fobb'd off thus by an old methodical piece
of clock-work, by a stiff starcht limb of the law, a
cutter of goose quills, and a scraper of parchments?
No: Evacuate my chamber. Tell your principal
I'll none of his advice; I value his opinion not a
rush: Shall I be taught and tutor'd at these years?

I'm

I'm fure I am an older man, and I believe a wifer than himfelf—fo tell him, Mafter Frampton.

FRAMPTON.
Have you no other commands for me than thefe?

NIGHTSHADE.
Pooh!

FRAMPTON.
I am your obedient—Good evening to your honour.

[*Exit.*

NIGHTSHADE.
Now why the devil won't that fellow be in a paf-fion? he'll no more be put out of his temper, than a German poftillion will out of his pace—So, Gregory! what news? have you found out the attorney?

S C E N E   V.

Enter G R E G O R Y.

GREGORY.
Your honour fhall hear the whole proceeding: At Thavies-Inn I firft got fcent of him, threw off, and took the drag as far as Shoe-Lane; there he hung cover; I had a warm burft to the Fleet; hunted him thro' Turn-again-Lane to the Old-Bailey; got an entapis, and run into him in Labour-in-vain-Court, Old Fifh-Street-Hill——

NIGHTSHADE.
Well, and what fays he to the profecution?

GREGORY.
For fome time he faid nothing; for when I firft arrived he was on a vifit to a friend under fentence of death in Newgate: however, after a while he came home, and then——

NIGHTSHADE.
What faid he then? to the point, Dunce.

GREGORY.
Why he faid, an pleafe your honour, he wou'd have nothing to do with the bufinefs: There's no credit to be got by fuch profecutions; if it had been

on

on a criminal indictment indeed—but he won't be concern'd in any vexatious fuit about game; humanity
won't fuffer him.

NIGHTSHADE.

Humanity indeed! was ever the like heard? But,
Sirrah, this is all a lie of your own inventing, and
your bones fhall anfwer for it. (*Threatening to cane him.*

SCENE VI.

STAPLETON, *and* NIGHTSHADE.

STAPLETON.

Keep the peace, in the King's name! what's the
matter now, friend Andrew?

NIGHTSHADE.

Why this fot would fain have me believe that a
Newgate folicitor will refufe a fuit upon motives of
humanity: A likely tale indeed! He comes home
from the fociety of a condemn'd malefactor, and
fcruples levying the penalty againft a poaching parfon. What would the noblemen and gentlemen, affo-
ciated for the prefervation of our game, fay to that?

STAPLETON.

Who cares what they would fay! What have men
of bufinefs to do with fuch difputes?

NIGHTSHADE.

Men of bufinefs! I have no bufinefs: I left off
trade, thank heaven, in time: You'll ftay till it has
left off you.

STAPLETON.

Why fo? Our warehoufes are as full, our com-
miffions as many, our credit as good as ever: What
do you fee about us makes you prophecy fo ill?

NIGHTSHADE.

I tell you, Sir, your trade is ebbing faft away from
you in every quarter of the globe. Look out and
fatisfy yourfelf; but I have done, 'tis no concern of
mine—What are your treaties with the Portuguefe?
waſte

waſte paper; linings for old trunks to carry home
the, refuſe goods, that they return upon your hands.
Another man would flatter you; but I'm your friend;
I let you know theſe things in time.

STAPLETON.

A moſt conſiderate precaution, truly.

NIGHTSHADE.

I have now no leiſure for converſations of this nature, but I would aſk a thinking man, what muſt be
the fate of your Turkey trade? Undone. You've
burnt their ſhips it ſeems, now you may burn your
own; you'll have no further call for them, unleſs you
ſend them to your colonies, to air your goods, and ex-
erciſe your ſailors—but I've ſomething elſe to think
of—Gregory, my hat! I'm ſtaying here too long.
Your ſervant, Mr. Stapleton—remember I have told
you now, I've let you know your danger——

STAPLETON.

And in the tendereſt manner; you are the kindeſt
friend: If we are ruin'd, you'll have nothing to regret
—Your ſervant—we ſhall meet again at ſupper——

NIGHTSHADE.

I juſt ſtep back to tell you that your weavers are
all riſing: I fell in with a large party of them in the
ſtreets: Your people migrating by thouſands: What!
men muſt not ſtarve.—I hint this to you gently, and
in pure good will; I have no intereſt to ſerve—and ſo
your ſervant for an hour or two—I'll tell you more
when I return—Oh, if I was a man to turn the gloomy
ſide of things upon you, I could draw a melancholly
picture truly!   [Exit.

STAPLETON.

The man who tells me a diſtaſteful lye, in ſome ſort
may be ſaid to recommend the truth; but he who,
like old Nightſhade, makes the truth offenſive, recom-
mends a lye.   [Exit.

SCENE

SCENE VII.

LÆTITIA, and LUCY.

LÆTITIA.

Lucy, come hither—you have a brother, I think, who is one of Counsellor Manlove's clerks.

LUCY.

I have, madam; and tho' I say it, as promising, genteel, well-spoken a young man as you would wish to set your eyes on; he is my only brother, ma'am.

LÆTITIA.

Let that be an excuse for your forwardness. I am not enquiring into his character.

LUCY.

If you did, ma'am, I assure you it will stand the strictest enquiry; my papa gave both of us an education—

LÆTITIA.

Your papa! let it be father in your mouth, if I might advise you.

LUCY.

Humph!—There's a person wants to speak with you.

LÆTITIA.

What person?

LUCY.

A person from abroad; a painting man, I believe; he says he has a recommendation to you—there are many such call here.

LÆTITIA.

If he has any letter of recommendation, desire he will be pleased to send it in. (*Exit Lucy.*) I cannot reconcile myself to this methodical course of proceeding; in the name of all that's happy, let our inclinations get the start of our proposals: If I could meet this Mr. Manlove naturally, and without form; if we

were

were then to fingle out each other by the guidance of no other monitor than the heart, and if a thoufand ifs befides were all to prove realities, a happy alliance might fucceed; but to be turn'd into a room to undergo the profeft furvey of a man, who comes upon a vifit of liking, is infupportably humiliating. It may well be faid of fome fathers, that they drive a fmithfield bargain for their daughters, when with butcherlike infenfibility they fhew 'em out for fale like cattle in a market.   (*Lucy returns.*)

LUCY.

The gentleman prefents his refpeefts to you, and defires you to perufe this letter; I think he is altogether as perfonable a young man as I would wifh to fee.   (*Gives the letter.*)

LÆTITIA.

Sure you forget yourfelf—let me fee—from Counfellor Manlove!—what is this?

Madam,

The bearer of this letter, is a young man in whofe profperity I am warmly interefted. He is lately return'd from Italy, where he has made fome proficiency in the art of which you are a miftrefs; and as I flatter myfelf you will find him not unworthy, I beg leave to recommend him to your protection and efteem. When my nephew has the honour of being known to you, he can give you fuller fatisfaction in this young man's particular than I can; in the mean time I venture to add, that Mr. Manlove will confider every favour you beftow, in this inftance, as conferr'd upon himfelf. I have the honour to be, Madam,

Your moft obedient, and moft humble Servant,

CHARLES MANLOVE, *Sen.*

Where is the gentleman? introduce him directly.
(LUCY *goes out, and brings in* CHARLES.
Your humble fervant, Sir: You are the gentleman referr'd to in this letter——

CHARLES.

CHARLES.

I am the perfon, Madam. What a lovely young woman! (*afide.*

LÆTITIA.

You are lately from Italy: Where did you principally purfue your ftudies?

CHARLES.

At Rome: I vifited Florence, Bologna, Venice and other places; but I regard Rome as the grand repofitory of the antique, and for that reafon I made my principal refidence there.

LÆTITIA.

To what branch of the art did you chiefly direct your attention?

CHARLES.

To the ftudy of beauty, Madam; and that in its fimpleft forms: A Laocoon, a Hercules, or a Caracalla may aftonifh; but it is a Fauftina, a Venus, an Apollo that delights, that ravifhes—But I am fpeaking to you on a fubject of which you are both by art a miftrefs, and an example by nature.

LÆTITIA.

Upon my word! (*afide.*) Come, Sir; we are here in the way of the family: allow me to fhew you into another apartment. (*She ftops.*) Was young Mr. Manlove at Rome when you was?

CHARLES.

He was.

LÆTITIA.

I underftand he has a very great regard for you.

CHARLES.

I hope I fhall not forfeit his good opinion.

LÆTITIA.

It does you much honour: All the world fpeaks highly of Mr. Manlove. I'll fhew you the way.

CHARLES.

Charming girl! I am in love with her at firft fight.

[*Exeunt.*

LUCY,

LUCY.

So, fo! a very promifing beginning. As fure as can be there's fomething in the wind about this Manlove: I fufpect the letter to be a fetch; and as for this painter, I am miftaken, if he is not fome how or other in the fecret—'tis a mighty pretty fellow.— Ah, brother Dibble, I am glad to fee you. How goes the world with you?

SCENE VIII.

LUCY, and DIBBLE.

DIBBLE.

Bufily, my girl, bufily. I have borrowed a moment's time from company to run to you: I have luckily found you alone: Utter not a word; be all attention: Jack Nightfhade, the country boy I made acquaintance with laft year, is now in town; but not a word of that—He is at a tavern hard by, with fome lads of mettle, who pufh about the glafs. What fay you, Huffey, to a bold ftroke for a hufband?

LUCY.

For a hufband! You are joking.

DIBBLE.

Serious, upon my honour! Oh, when the blood begins to boil, and the brain begins to turn, every thing may be attempted. He has fignified to me that he is in want of a wife; you, I fuppofe, have no objection to a hufband; fo far you are both of a mind. He fays the lady muft be rich; the condition is a reafonable one; and you muft provide a forttne for the purpofe: What fay you to your miftrefs's? He vifits you in the name of Mr. Manlove; why may not you receive him in that of Mifs Fairfax?

LUCY.

Impoffible! Don't you know his father lodges in this very houfe?

F   DIE-

DIBBLE.

Scare boys with bug-bears: I have provided againſt
danger; and with a promiſe of a good round ſum,
upon the wedding night, have made old Gregory my
own: He will aid our projeĉt, and keep watch upon
old Surly-boots, I warrant you.

LUCY.

But what is gain'd, if we ſhou'd compaſs our ends ?
the young man is a minor, and his father wou'd diſ-
inherit him.

DIBBLE.

Fear nothing—he's of age—Gregory confirms it:
And as for his father's diſinheriting him, I'll tell you
a ſecret; it is not in his power: When the Counſellor
ſettled an eſtate on Charles, old Nightſhade cut him
off with a ſhilling, and gave his fortune to Jack: I
drew the deed myſelf; it is as tight as law can tye it.

LUCY.

I don't know what to ſay; a ſettlement to be ſure
is ſomething; Mrs. Nightſhade and an equipage, is
better than plain Lucy and a pair of pattens: But
then my heart miſgives me—and the boy, they ſay, is
ſuch a cub——

DIBBLE.

Fine airs, in truth! Nay, if you are ſo exceptious,
pleaſe yourſelf; it's no affair of mine; I've done
with it.

LUCY.

Hold, hold; you are ſo touchy if one ſpeaks—
My madam will be monſtrous angry, but no matter.
Yeſterday was married John Nightſhade, Eſq. to
Miſs——O, Gemini, 'twill make a flaming daſh !|

DIBBLE.

Ay, ay, leave me to draw the marriage deed; I'll
jointure you I warrant. Come, decide; time's precious, and the moment ſerves: Old Nightſhade's
out; the ladies too, I underſtand, are on the wing—
When ſhall we come ?

LUCY.

L U C Y.

When? I don't know—I vow I'm half afraid—Is there no law againſt me, if I am caught, and the ſcheme fails?

D I B B L E.

Pſhaw! you are ſo irreſolute; ev'n be a ſervant-maid all days of your life; I care not.

L U C Y.

No, brother; I've as much ambition as my betters, ſo here's my hand—I'm with you—give me half an hour's time to con my leſſon and I'll be ready for you.

D I B B L E.

That's my brave girl! Courage! the day's our own. If every thing's in train, and the coaſt clear, let Gregory meet us at the corner of the ſtreet, ex-aⅽtly in half an hour's time. But, hark'ee, Lucy; Jack is incog, and takes his brother Manlove's name, remember that: By the way, I ſuſpeⅽt ſomething's in the wind between your Madam and Mr. Charles.

L U C Y.

Why ſo?

D I B B L E.

Becauſe I ſaw him turn into her room juſt now, in an undreſs; he paſs'd me on the ſtairs, and whiſper'd me in the ear, not to open my lips concerning his being here to a ſingle ſoul, for my life; therefore make no miſchief—Farewel, I muſt be gone. [Exit.

L U C Y.

Your humble ſervant, virtuous Miſs Lætitia Fair-fax; your painter then, as I ſuſpeⅽted, turns out a lover in diſguiſe; and you, it ſeems, have your in-trigues as well as other folks. Who wou'd be nice about charaⅽter in theſe times, when all the world conſpires to put virtue out of countenance, and keep viⅽe in?

ACT

A C T   III.

SCENE I. *A Room in Stapleton's House.*

NIGHTSHADE, *and* STAPLETON.

NIGHTSHADE.

AND so you'll positively ship those bales of Norwich Crape for Holland?

STAPLETON.
I purpose so to do.

NIGHTSHADE.
You purpose so to do! and the Kersies and Callimancoes and Perpetuanoes too I warrant.

STAPLETON.
I do.

NIGHTSHADE.
The devil you do! I tell you what then, Master Stapleton, they will not have their name for nothing; you'll find them Perpetuanoes on your hands: I'd send tea to America as soon. Why sure I understand the Dutch markets; sure I think I do; you've found I understood them.

STAPLETON.
But times are altered, brother Andrew.

NIGHTSHADE.
With the devil to 'em. Times are alter'd truly, and trade is alter'd, and merchants are alter'd and grown obstinate blockheads, deaf to good counsel, ignorant of their business; a frivolous, gossiping, pleasure hunting crew; forsaking their counters for their country-houses, Change for Change-alley.—What sort of a season at Newfoundland? have you ship'd your fish yet for the Mediteranian-markets?

But

But what is it all to me? I have wound up my bottom: 'Twas a noble hit, Master Stapleton, that speculation of mine in saltpetre.

STAPLETON.

I believe it turn'd to tolerable account.

NIGHTSHADE.

I believe it did; I may venture to assue you it did, to tolerable account, as you say, tho'.you predicted otherwise; it made my pillow for me; yes, yes, thank heaven, I'm easy; I've laid down my cares.

STAPLETON.

And taken up content. What a happy fellow are you, friend Andrew!

NIGHTSHADE.

But I tell you you're mistaken, I am not a happy fellow; I would not be thought happy; the world's too wicked for an honest man to be happy or contented in it.

STAPLETON.

But you are out of the world; you are settled in a peaceful retreat, in rural tranquillity, cultivating your own acres, enjoying your own produce.

NIGHTSHADE.

Blood and fire, I tell you other people are enjoying my produce; my servants are embezzeling my property, my neighbours are destroying my game, the vermin are laying waste my granaries, and the rot is making havock with my sheep; and how the vengeance then can I be happy?

STAPLETON.

By bearing every thing with a patient mind.

NIGHTSHADE.

Patient! I am patient to a fault.

STAPLETON.

By reflecting, when your servants or neighbours molest you, what an examplary young man you are blest with for a son.

NIGHT-

NIGHTSHADE.
Yes, yes, the boy's as good as his neighbours.

STAPLETON.
I never heard fo univerfal a good charcter.

NIGHTSHADE.
'Tis a fober, frugal lad, that's the truth on't.

STAPLETON.
So accomplifh'd a genius, fo diftinguifh'd a tafte for the fine arts.

NIGHTSHADE.
For the fine arts! that's rather too much, I know no art Jack has but fetting trimmers, worming puppies, and making fowling nets.　　*(afide.*

STAPLETON.
Your fon, friend Addrew, is not like the prefent frippery race of young men; he is a man of found principle and good morals; no libertine, no free-thinker, no gamefter.

NIGHTSHADE.
Gamefter indeed! I'd game him, with the devil to him.

STAPLETON.
He has more elegant refources: The woman muft be happy who can engage his affections.

NIGHTSHADE.
I wifh your ward Mifs Fairfax was of your opinion.

STAPLETON.
Are you fincere?

NIGHTSHAE.
Why to be fure I am. Don't I know fne'll have a very confiderable fortune?

STAPLETON.
A fig for her fortune—here's my hand—fo the young folks can like each other, and Mr. Manlove is confenting——

NIGHT-

NIGHTSHADE.

Who? who is confenting? Mr. Manlove?

STAPLETON.

Ay furely; I'm afraid we do not rightly underftand, each other: Which of your fons are you fpeaking of?

NIGHTSHADE.

Which of my fons am I fpeaking of! the only one I ever do fpeak of; the only one which I acknowledge, Jack. You cou'dn't think me fuch a fool to recommend that puppily pig-tail'd ape, with his effences and pulvilios; that monkey, whom my filly brother fent to fee the world, with his grand tour, and his pictures, and his impertinencies? No— I tell you once for all, I've done with him; he has dropt my name and I my nature; let him that chriften'd him anew, keep him; I have done with him.

STAPLETON.

You fhock me to hear you fay fo.

NIGHTSHADE.

What; fhan't I fpeak of my own fon as I think fit?

STAPLETON.

Yes, if you fpeak as a father fhou'd.

NIGHTSHADE.

And who's the judge of that? Have you a fon? Are you a father? No, you are a guardian: Heaven help the poor young woman that's your ward. Marry her to Charles Manlove! marry her to her garters fooner, and tye her up upon the curtain rod, 'twere a better deed. And what know you of the fine arts? Are you a painter as well as your ward here? I fee no tokens of it; the London 'Prentice, and the March to Finchley, feem to be the fum total of your collection—His tafte, it feems, has captivated you; his tafte for what? for Camblets, for Cafoys, for Manchefter and Norwich commodities? There lies your learning; thofe are your univerfities.

STAPLE-

STAPLETON.

Andrew Nightshade, Andrew Nightshade, recollect yourself: We'll converse when you are cool: I talk to no man in a passion.

NIGHTSHADE.

I in a passion? 'Tis the first time I was ever told so, and shall be the last, from you at least—Here, Gregory, where are you: —I'll be gone this instant; I'll have my things pack'd up; I'll rid your house, at least, of one passionate man. I in a passion? I that never lost my temper—But your servant, Sir; your servant, Mr. Stapleton: Perhaps you'll say I'm in a passion now. Here, Gregory! why Gregory!

[*Exit.*

STAPLETON (*alone.*)

Ha, ha, ha! of a certain, Andrew, thou'rt a ridiculous old fellow. If I had an acquaintance with the poets, I would get them to exhibit thy humours on the stage; 'twould be a diverting scene, and no bad moral.

Enter Mrs. STAPLETON *and* LÆTITIA.

Mrs. STAPLETON.

Here's a fine storm; he's calling for his servants to pack up his things; he vows he'll quit the house immediately.

LÆTITIA.

A happy resolution. What a snapdragon it is! No Yorkshire housewife in her washing-week can be more peevish.

Mrs. STAPLETON.

I wish he was out of the house; I cannot bear to have your peace annoy'd.

STAPLETON.

My peace! You have had a visitor, Lætitia.

LÆTITIA.

A brother artist, and a friend of Mr. Manlove's, I declare I've lost my heart to him.

STAPLE-

STAPLETON.

Then I deny that he's a friend of Mr. Manlove's.

LÆTITIA.

Oh, Sir, he is the prettiest man! so candid, so intelligent; full of his art, and glowing warm with all that taste for the antique, which true genius is sure to gain by travel.

STAPLETON.

Ay, ay, I understand you; he's been praising your performances.

LÆTITIA.

I own it; but what flatters me above all, he commends your portrait exceedingly; I shall proceed in it with twice the spirit I began.

Mrs. STAPLETON.

He has turned her head with flattery; the grace of Raphael, the design of Michael Angelo, Titian's warmth, and Corregio's beauty, centre all in her un-rivall'd compositions!

STAPLETON.

Hey-day! where learnt you all this gabble? here's a pack of names for a citizen's wife to get by heart.

Mrs. STAPLETON.

Do you think I've clean'd her pallet then for nothing? The doctor's Merry-andrew knows the names of his drugs, or he's not fit for his place. We are going this instant upon a visit of virtu to Mr. Manlove's: This young painter speaks in raptures of his collection: He has some pictures, which are said to be inimitable.

LÆTITIA.

Dear Sir, I hope you've no objection. He has talk'd to me so much of a Lucretia by Guido, that I am dying to visit her.

STAPLETON.

I shou'd doubt if Lucretia wou'd do as much for you. I hardly think this visit is in rule.

G   LÆTITIA:

LÆTITIA.

It is done every day; half the town has been there:
I go there as a ftudent—befides, Mrs. Stapleton goes
with me.

STAPLETON.

Well, well, I am no critic in thefe matters, entertain yourfelves and you have my free leave. Much
pleafure to you both—your fervant. [*Exit*.

LÆTITIA.

Come, my dear madam, the light ftill ferves us;
let us lofe no time. [*Exeunt*.

SCENE II. *The Painting Room.*

Enter LUCY.

LUCY.

Now the duce fetch this madcap brother of mine,
what a twitter has he thrown me into! I can fettle to
nothing: Madam and her fham-painter have made a
fine diforder in this room. I don't know any ufe
thefe geniufes are of, but to put every thing out of
its place. Ah! is it you?

Enter DIBBLE

DIBBLE.

Hufh, hufh! compofe yourfelf; you had like to
have ruin'd all: Why didn't you fend Gregory to the
ftreet's end, as you agreed?

LUCY.

Lud, I'm in fuch a flutter—I don't know, I'm
frighted. Is he here?

DIBBLE.

Ready: Prim'd high with brifk Champagne: The
train'd is laid; you have the fire; touch it, and off
it goes.

LUCY.

Fire! I've no fire about me. Did the fervants fee
you?

DIB.

DIBBLE.

No; Gregory let us in, and has the young 'Squire now in keeping: There never was fo fortunate a moment. Hark! he's at the door.

JACK. *(from without)*

Hift! Lawyer—Pickle—Bully-Jack!——fhall I come in?

DIBBLE.

He muft come in; flip out a moment 'till I prepare him, and then—Remember, Lucy, he is Mr. Manlove here, and yourfelf Lætitia. Go your ways. *(Exit Lucy.)* Now, my lad of glory, I fhall fhow you a phænomenon, a ftar of the firft water.

Enter JACK.

JACK.

Water! I fcorn it: Give me wine: There's honefty in that, and wit and love. I'm monftroufly in love —but where's the lady?

DIBBLE.

Oh, fhe's at hand, and half your own already. I've been preaching to her—Mifs, fays I——

JACK.

Rot your *fays I!* who cares for what you fay: Show me the girl: I want no lawyer in this cafe; Champagne's my counfellor. You are a blockhead, Dibble, and a flincher: I'm for all the game; fee'd on both fides, boy; a bottle in my right hand, and a bottle in my left; double-charg'd, at heart and head; one for courage and t'other for invention. Pooh! my brother's a fool to me; his coat was never in fuch company before. Where is the lady, I fay? I muft fee the lady.

DIBBLE.

Well, well, be patient; you fhall fee the lady. [*Exit.*

JACK.

Ay, this puts every thing in motion: Now the world goes round: It has found its legs at laft, and dances

like

like Plough-Monday.   Drown it, 'twas afleep before.
What's all this lumber for *(ftumbling over the Eafel)*
The devil! who are you? *(fpeaking to the Layman)*
what's your profeffion?   An eafy, flender, dangling
figure, and as much of a gentleman as moft you fhall
meet.—The piggins! now 1 fmoak the jeft: She
paints. Oh damn it! fhe's an artift—That won't do;
there's no ftanding that; I muft overturn all this
trumpery: I fhall foon tumble you out of the room,
my dear—your reign's a fhort one, take my word.
Ay, here fhe comes!

Enter D I B B L E *with* L U C Y.

D I B B L E.
Mr. Manlove, this is Mifs Fairfax.   Mifs, this is
Mr. Manlove.

J A C K.
Madam, behold the fondeft of your flaves. My
friend here Lawyer Dibble has inform'd you that my
name is Manlove, and he tells me you are call'd Mifs
Fairfax.   Be it fo; if he tells a lie, he is not the firft
of his profeffion who has fo done. If you fhould think
that I am ratherelevated and in the air, I won't deny it;
Champagne, you know, is a fearching liquor, and my
fcull is none of the deepeft; but if you fuppofe that I
am fo blind as to overlook your beauties, or my own
perfections, you are not the perfon I take you for.
Dibble, come hither, make the Lady acquainted with
fome of my good qualities.   Difcufs.

L U C Y.
Oh, Sir, what need? the good qualities of Mr.
Manlove are in every body's mouth.

J A C K.
Deuce take me now, if that is any flattery to me.

D I B B L E.
I told you, Madam, what a modeft young gentleman he was.

JACK.

JACK.

Oh, you're a precious devil.   Be pleas'd to tell the Lady likewife what a brave eftate I have got; fuch things come naturally from a lawyer's mouth; tell her what it is, and where it lies: Drown me, if I know where to find an acre of it.

LUCY,

Oh, never name eftate when Mr. Manlove's in the cafe: Your perfon, air, addrefs——

JACK,

Madam, you do me honour.   'Egad, I fhall have no occafion for courtfhip.   (*afide.*)

LUCY.

Your genius, tafte, accomplifhments—I myfelf have fome fmall turn for painting—

JACK.

Yes, and I fhould like you as well without it. (*afide,*

LUCY.

But you, I dare fay, are a mafter-hand; and poetry, no doubt, is full as much your own.

JACK.

Faith, there's not much to choofe between 'em.

LUCY.

But then your education—one may fee that you have travell'd.

DIBBLE.

Oh, yes, that's very vifible.

JACK.

Well faid, lawyer—She has a damnable clack.

LUCY,

I fhould be delighted to hear an account of your travels: I dare fay you have met many fingular adventures.

JACK.

A thoufand; but I have taken an oath never to fpeak of 'em.

LUCY.

LUCY.

Oh, you muſt conquer ſuch ſcruples. What advantages has your uncle's bounty given you, Mr,
Manlove, over that poor lad in the country!

JACK.

And yet I'd rather hear one kind word ſaid of that
poor lad in the country, than a whole volume of Mr.
Manlove's praiſes. I'm hipp'd, whenever I hear the
ſubject mentioned.

DIBBLE.

Make up to him, Lucy, or he's loſt. Jack Nightſhade, what are you about? one bold attack, and ſhe's
your own.

JACK.

It may be ſo; but you muſt know I have a kind of
partiality for that ſame country lubber, Jack Nightſhade; and 'till I can find a Lady, who will prefer him
to his brother, I will remain as I am; ſo there's an end
of the matter, d'ye ſee, and no harm done. Madam,
I'm your ſervant. [Exit.

LUCY.

So finiſhes the chapter of huſbands. I thank you,
for your ſcheme.

DIBBLE.

Thank yourſelf for your folly. What poſſeſt you
with the thought of touching upon the lad in the
country? how could you be ſo flippant?

LUCY.

What does it ſignify? He is too cunning to be
caught with chaff; e'en drop your project.

DIBBLE.

No, let deſpair go hang. I am not eaſily repuls'd:
Take courage, and commit yourſelf to me; I have
reſources yet you know not of. Come, Lucy, you
ſhall ſee my genius riſes on defeat. [Exeunt.

SCENE III. Manlove's Houſe.

CHARLES. (Alone.)

It is time to take off the maſk; I have ſeen and
heard enough: She who can captivate both eyes and

ears

ears at once, is irrefiftable; Mifs Fairfax is fo com-
pos'd, that fhe has beauty enough to blind our under-
ftandings, if fhe wanted wit; and wit enough to blind
our eyes, if fhe wanted beauty.   I will go to her in
this habit once again, and folicit an inteiview for Mr.
Manlove: If fhe readily grants it, I will avail myfelf
of her compliance, and inftantly difclofe myfelt—if
not—But what, in the name of wonder, have we got
here: Ha, ha, ha! my Paris fuit, by all that's brilliant;
the very *chef d'œuvre* of the fuperlative Monf. Le Duc:
That coat was made for grand occafions; it efcorted
me to the nuptials of the great Count d'Artois; it has
now the honour to attend the revels of the illuftrious
Jack Nightfhade.

Enter J A C K.
J A C K

Ay, and had I been willing, it might have affifted
at another wedding: 'Egad, it might have carried off
a fine girl, and one of the firft fortunes in the city.

C H A R L E S.

I fhould have thought your fcenes had rather laid
amongft the girls of freedom, than of fortune.

J A C K.

This lady, Sir, had both.   Swear to me you'll be
fecret, and I'll tell you where I've been.

C H A R L E S.

Nay, Jack, you'll truft me fure without an oath;
you know I am no tell-tale.   Where have you been?

J A C K.

You'll fcarce believe it; where on all this earth
but to the very houfe, where old Surlyboots fets up
his reft!

C H A R L E S.

To Mr. Stapleton's?

J A C K.

To the enemies head quarters: A high ftroke!

C H A R L E S.

And what carried you thither?

JACK.

JACK.

A girl: The wench I told you of.

CHARLES.

But what fort of a wench? I don't underftand how any girl could carry you to Mr. Stapleton's.

JACK.

No! She'd have carried me any where; all the world over: She is ready to fet out on her travells.

CHARLES.

And her name is——

JACK.

Fairfax.

CHARLES.

How!

JACK.

Lætitia Fairfax.

CHARLES.

What is it you have been doing? I am much interefted in this lady's good opinion, and if you have done or faid any thing to offend her——

JACK.

Offend her! Zooks, if you had heard how mere a country whelp fhe made of me, you wou'd own I had moft reafon to be offended of the two.

CHARLES.

Still I don't underftand you; you tell your ftory fo confufedly, I can make out nothing from it.

JACK.

Tell it yourfelf then, brother.

CHARLES.

But this precaution I muft give you, Jack, not to go upon that ground again; keep your fallies within proper bounds, and direct them to proper objects. Mifs Fairfax is a lady for whom I have the tendereft efteem; have a care therefore, young man, how you affront her as you value my refentment.

JACK.

Whuh!

Enter

Enter FREDERICK.

FREDERICK.

Sir, Mr. Manlove requeſts your company at his chambers immediately.

CHARLES.

I attend him—Brother, I am ſerious—Hitherto I hope no miſchief has been done; but I expeĉt that you obſerve what I have told you, and be more prudent for the future.   [*Exit.*

JACK.

And be a prig like you—Oh, you ſhall ſmart for this; I'll curry your fine hide. Now would I give both ears from off this head, if I could make the girl but fairly jilt this puppy, and revenge myſelf upon him.

Enter DIBBLE.

DIBBLE.

Squire!

JACK.

Ah, Dibble, I have made myſelf a precious blockhead.

DIBBLE.

What, in the penitentials? Is the Champagne cloudy?

JACK.

Vexation ſobers me like a wet napkin. Oh, if I cou'd ſee the girl again!

DIBBLE.

Do you wiſh it?

JACK.

Wiſh it! I'd crawl to Scotland on my knees; nay more, I'd live rhere all my days, ſo I could bilk this elder brother with Miſs Fairfax.

DIBBLE.

Say you ſo, Squire? This betters my beſt hopes. Follow me once more to Mr. Stapleton's: Take courage, and my life upon't the lady is your own.

JACK.

Have with you then; I'm ready; come along.

H   DIB-

DIBBLE.

Hold, not fo faft—the old lion may be in his den,
Give me one quarter of an hour's law, and then if we
mifcarry, crop thefe ears and nail them up like vermin
to your walls.

JACK.

Agreed! I take you at your word.   (*Exit Dibble.*)
Now, my fine brother, if I catch you on the hip I'll
give your pride a fall; I'll fhew you that a clown may
have a courtier's cunning.   Hey-day! who comes
here?

Mrs. STAPLETON *and* LÆTITIA, *ufher'd
in by* FREDERICK.

FREDERICK.

I beg pardon, Sir, I thought you was gone out:
Thefe ladies are defirous of feeing the pictures, and
I was conducting them to the room—

JACK.

I will take that honour on myfelf.   Go before and
open the windows.   (*Exit Fred.*)   You are fond of
paintings, ladies; I am glad it is in my power to
entertain you.

Mrs. STAPLETON.

You are the owner, Sir, of this admirable collection.
Your name is Manlove.

JACK.

At the fervice of the ladies always.   I'll pafs a few
of lawyer Dibble's airs upon them—I'm in a rare
cue.   (*afide.*)

LÆTITIA.

What do they mean by talking up this young man?
He has a miferable addrefs: I fee very little of the
man of fafhion about him.

Mrs. STAPLETON.

I cannot fay much for his perfon to be fure.

JACK.

She has fixt her eyes upon me; fhe is taken with
my perfon and addrefs—Don't you find it rather cold,
ladies?

adies ? —I wish there was a fire in the room, that I might give her a taste of my breeding.···· *(aside:)*

LÆTITIA.

The public is much bound to you for giving them access to your collection.

JACK.

If the public found no more amusement in them than I do, they might hang in the dark till doom's-day.

LÆTITIA.

You jest, I believe : Is it possible, after taking such pains in procuring them, you can have no enjoyment in the possession of them ?

JACK.

Even so, Madam; they resemble matrimony in that respect; the pursuit is the pleasure. But come, ladies, the room is ready, and I'll shew you the way.— What the devil does that old Duenna come for ?

(Goes out.)

LÆTITIA.

Is this the accomplish'd Mr. Manlove ? He seems in a strange humour: Are you sure he is perfectly sober ? I declare I scarce like to follow him.

JACK *(returns.)*

Ladies, this is the way : Indulge me with the honour of your hand. *(leads out Lætitia)* [*Exeunt.*

SCENE III.

An Apartment magnificently furnished with pictures.

JACK *introducing Mrs.* STAPLETON *and* LÆTITIA.

JACK.

There, Ladies ; there they hang: A jolly crew of 'em. Old Ladies in furrs and furbelows up to their throats, and young ones without a rag to cover 'em : These painters are but scurvy taylors ; they'll send a goddess into the world without a cloud to cover her : There are some pretty conceits go with their histories, but they will speak for themselves ; I am but little in their secrets.

H 2 .   LÆTITIA.

LÆTITIA.

What a blaze of beauty! there's the *Titian* Venus; heavens! what a form! what brilliant hues! But look, dear Madam, here is grace and dignity; *Guido*'s Lucretia: the dagger in her breaft, and in the act of heroic felf-deftruction: What refolution! what a fpirit has the great artift thrown into thofe eyes!

JACK.

Yes, fhe had a devil of a fpirit: She ftabb'd her-felf in a pique upon being crofs'd in love.

Mrs. STAPLETON.

You prefume on our ignorance; hiftory, I believe, affigns more elevated motives for Lucretia's death.

JACK.

Very likely; there were great pains taken to fmother the ftory; but 'tis as I tell you—I had it from a near relation of the family.

LÆTITIA.

Ridiculous! Do you obferve that picture, Madam; 'tis a melancholly ftory, very finely told by Pouffin: It is a view of Marfeilles at the time of the plague, with a capital figure of the good bifhop in the midft of the groupe.

JACK

Bifhop, Madam! that perfon which you look up-on is a phyfician, and the people round about him are his patients; they are in a defperate way it muft be confeft. Do you fee that angry figure in the corner; he is a gamefter: he is picking lead out of loaded dice to run into bullets, to fire through his own head: 'Tis no bad moral.

LÆTITIA.

You are infinitely kind to favour us with thefe anecdotes: If you are thus gracious to all ftrangers, the world will edify abundantly. But we won't put you to the trouble of explanation—we are not en-tirely ignorant—tho' your collection may be the beft we have feen, it is not abfolutely the firft.

JACK.

Belike then you are a painter, as well as the lady I vifited juft now.

LÆTITIA.

LÆTITIA.

In the prefence of fuch mafters as are here affembled,
I cannot call myfelf a painter; in my own chamber I
fometimes perfuade myfelf I am.

JACK.

Yes, I am told it is an art which ladies moftly
practife in their own chambers — What fay you to that
picture over the door? 'tis a merry conceit.

LÆTITIA.

It is the colouring of the Venetian fchool; I fhould
guefs it to be *Tintoret.*

JACK.

Oh, you are quite out of the ftory.

Mrs. STAPLETON.

She is fpeaking of the mafter: The ftory is plainly
that of Actæon, and no bad moral; he was turn'd
into a ftag, by the goddefs of chaftity, for his im-
pertinent curiofity.

JACK.

Excufe me, Madam, you miftake the moral—
That gentleman with the antlers on his head, is a city
hufband, the principal lady in the fhow is his wife;
fhe wears a crefcent on her forehead to fignify fhe is a
dealer in horns; her companions are a groupe of city
Madams: The painter drew them bathing to fhew
the warmth of their conftitutions.

LÆTITIA.

Upon my word you have a great deal of wit, and
you have a fine collection of paintings; but one
capital piece is wanting.

JACK.

And what is that, pray?

LÆTITIA.

Modefty: It will be an excellent companion to your
Lucretia.

JACK.

But who fhall I get to fit for the likenefs?

LÆTITIA.

You will find it admirably painted by the fame
mafter. Come, Madam, it is time for us to be gone.

JACK.

JACK.

You are not for the city-end of the town, I conclude.

Mrs. STAPLETON.

Our home is in the city.

JACK.

Permit me to conduct you thither; I have a coach in waiting, and am bound to New Broad-Street, if you know such a place.

Mrs. STAPLETON.

Intimately; but we have a carriage of our own.

LÆTITIA.

Can there be any attractions in the city to engage Mr. Manlove's regards?

JACK.

Oh, yes; an assignation, Madam: I am loth to disappoint a fond girl.

LÆTITIA.

'Tis charitably consider'd.

JACK.

Nay, I don't know but I shou'd be inclined to take her for better for worse, if it was not for one circumstance in her disfavour.

LÆTITIA.

May I ask what that may be?

JACK.

She has a devilish itch for painting: I shou'd expect to have all my gods and goddesses taken down to make room for her vulgar friends and relations.

Mrs. STAPLETON.

Ay, that wou'd be a sorrowful exchange to my knowledge.

LÆTITIA.

Yes, have a care of that same painting girl: My life upon it she will slip through your hands.

JACK.

Why I have my eye upon that honest gentleman in the picture, with the stag's-horns, I must own— Who shall I tell her gave me the caution?

LÆTITIA.

No matter; when you see Miss Fairfax you'll remember me.

JACK.

JACK.

Fairfax! the vengeance: How came you to guefs
her name?

LÆTITIA.

Oh, Sir, there is but one painter in the ftreet, and
fhe, I believe, will remain there; your collection is
fafe; fhe will trouble you with none of her performances, none of her daubings, take my word. Your
moft obedient—Let us make hafte home, and be ready
to receive him: Vain, fenfelefs coxcomb! how I
fhall enjoy his confuffion! [*Exit with Mrs. Staple.*

JACK.

A good lively wench, but the devil of a tongue!
I'll run and hand her to her coach, [*Exit.*

ACT IV. SCENE I.

Enter DIBBLE *and* LUCY.

LUCY,

STILL I proteft againft your project; we fhall
reap nothing from it, take my word, but fhame and
difappointment; however, to convince you that my
fears are not for myfelf, I am prepared and fhall go
through with it, as you defire.

DIBBLE.

My life upon't, he takes the bait this time.

LUCY.

I doubt it, but no matter: Sure it's time that he
was come. Hark! who is that? look out.

DIBBLE.

'Sdeath! Mrs. Stapleton and Mifs Lætitia,

LUCY.

What's to be done now?

DIBBLE.

We've nothing for it, but a defperate fally; flip
the back-way down with me, and let us both go out
and

and ſtop young Nightſhade : We can take him to my
lodgings and prevent an interview that muſt be fatal.

LUCY.

It is too late to deliberate : Come on.   [*Exeunt.*

Enter Mrs. STAPLETON *and* LÆTITIA.

Mrs. STAPLETON.

Come, my dear Lætitia, you think of this affair
too ſeriouſly : You cannot much regret a man you
never ſaw before.

LÆTITIA.

It's true; and yet, with ſhame I own it to you, I
am mortified ſeverely. Was there ever ſuch a diſ-
appointment ?

Mrs. STAPLETON.

Either he treated us with inexcuſable contempt, or
is profoundly ignorant. Did you remark the ridiculous obſervations he made on ſome of the pictures ?

LÆTITIA.

Yes; but I ſet that down for miſtaken wit; in
ſhort, his manners are of the vulgareſt caſt. Are
theſe the fruits of public education ? Is this the finiſh'd
gentleman ? the ſcholar ? traveller ?—His booriſh
brother in the country cannot outgo this : And the
world to be ſo blinded ! Oftentimes it ſpeaks worſe of
a man than he deſerves ; it is ſeldom guilty of telling
ſo many untruths in his favour.

Enter SERVANT.

SERVANT.

A gentleman deſires to ſpeak with Miſs Fairfax.

LÆTITIA.

'Tis he—Conduct him into the drawing-room ; I'll
wait on him immediately.   [*Exit Ser.*

Mrs. STAPLETON.

Well, Lætitia, I need not recommend to you to
treat him as he deſerves.

LÆTITIA.

I muſt be more, or leſs, than a woman, if I ſpar'd
him.   [*Exeunt ſeverally.*
SCENE

SCENE II.

SERVANT *introducing* JACK NIGHTSHADE.

SERVANT.

Pleafe to walk in here, Sir; Mifs Fairfax will wait on you immediately. · [*Exit.*

JACK.

Ay, ay; I dare fay fhe will: Egad, there's no time to be loft—Drown it, where's Dibble? I expected he wou'd meet me at the gate: If I fhou'd ftumble on old Crufty—I don't like the looks of the land fo well as I did: Here's fuch a folitude, and fuch a ceremony—Why the plague do they make me kick my heels here? What, the vengeance! is fhe come again?

Enter LÆTITIA.

LÆTITIA.

Your humble fervant, Mr. Manlove: You fcarce expected, I believe, to meet your vifitor again fo foon.

JACK.

No, indeed: it is vaftly beyond my hopes.

LÆTITIA.

You are punctual to your affignation, I perceive.

JACK.

Oh yes, Ma'am: to be fure, Ma'am—How the plague fhall I get rid of her?

LÆTITIA.

You did well to confider the poor fond girl that is dying for you.

JACK.

She has the devil of an affurance—What are thefe London Ladies made of?

LÆTITIA.

He is thoroughly confounded: I'll give him a chance, however.—Have you any commands for me, Sir?

JACK.

Commands! Oh, none in life, I thank you; no commands. What won't that ferve? No: She will

I   have

have her talk out at least. I hope you lik'd the
pictures? Sure Miss Fairfax will come presently.

LÆTITIA.

I admire your collection greatly; my expectations
in that particular were not disappointed.

JACK.

I understand your insinuation, Madam; but Ladies
expectations, I am told, are not always to be satisfied.

LÆTITIA.

In Mr. Manlove's instance, perhaps not easily.

JACK.

Really, Madam, I shou'd wish to do justice to a
lady's good opinion: but your visit, I must say, was
rather unseasonable, and that elderly Lady was so
vexatiously in the way.

LÆTITIA.

I am sorry for it, Sir: I am afraid our visit was
rather out of rule.

JACK.

That's honest now; and since you own it, I must
fairly say, the present is none of the most welcome.

LÆTITIA.

I readily believe it—and therefore, Sir, though it
is not altogether in character for me to promote a
conversation of such a sort as you hinted at when we
met at your own house; yet, I must observe to you,
if you have any such proposal in design, it will be for
both our ease that you shou'd come to the point directly.

JACK.

To the point, Madam! Upon my soul I don't
know what to say to that—To be sure I did come
here with a full and fixt design of offering myself to
Miss Fairfax upon the marrying lay, and that, you
know, at best is but a hanging kind of job; so that
if I appear rather dull of apprehension, I hope you
will recollect that a man cannot be very merry when
he's on his road to his execution.

LÆTITIA.

Oh, Sir, be under no concern on that account;
assure yourself, I have to the full as little disposition
towards that state as you can have.

JACK.

JACK.

Well faid again! but it won't take.—You are in the right; you are for enjoying your freedom.

LÆTITIA.

Since we are both agreed in that refpect, what occafion is there for more words? I believe we may break up the conference.

JACK.

As foon as ever you pleafe; I am by no means for delaying you.

LÆTITIA.

I wait your motions, Mr. Manlove, I'm here at home.

JACK.

You cannot be more fo than I am.

LÆTITIA.

Indeed! this conduct, Mr. Manlove, is fo oppofite to all that I expected from you, that I'm caft into aftonifhment. Upon what reafons, or from what caprice you've chofe to take it up I know not; natural it cannot be to any man. However, Sir, I'll take you at your word, and, for a moment, will fuppofe you more welcome in this houfe than you really are, and leave you in poffeffion of it. [*Exit.*

JACK.

Come, come, well off! I've bolted her at laft. 'Fore George, I begin to be tired of my plumes: Every man's beft in his own coat and his own character: Plain Jack and the country, wou'd have fuited me better: There are fo many demands upon a fine gentleman, that nobody but a fine gentleman can tell how to avoid them.

Enter **GREGORY.**

GREGORY.

Ah, Mafter Jacky, keep clofe. Yonder's your old Dadd at the ftreet door in a notable primmuniry.

JACK.

Death and the devil! how fhall I break pafture without his feeing me?

GREGORY.

Never fear it; he has a job upon his hands will

I 2   tether

tether him for one while.   Egad, I hope they'll trea
him with a ducking.

JACK.

What is the matter?

GREGORY.

Nay, nothing out of courfe; he has crack'd the
news-man's noddle for winding his horn in his ear;
he pretends to have delicate nerves, you know; and
fo the fellow rais'd a mob upon him, that has drove
him into cover, and they are now baying the old buck
at the door.   Ay, yonder he is; you muft keep clofe
till he's off his ftand.

JACK.

Have an eye upon the door—I hope they will fcare
him foundly; it may fave your fcull and mine many
a hard pelt.   But, Gregory, who is this fine Madam
I've been talking to?   Lawyer Dibble fure has not
put me on a wrong fcent: They introduc'd her to me
as Mifs Fairfax; are there two Mifs Fairfaxes, as well
as two Mr. Manloves; a falfe one and a true one?

GREGORY.

What fhall I fay now?—Oh, yes, there are two
ladies of that name; but this is only a coufin of the
other; a kind of hanger-on in the family.

JACK.

A hanger-on, do you fay?—Keep your eye upon
the door—Why, fhe's better drefs'd, and a finer woman than her I'm in purfuit of.

GREGORY.

Ay, ay, but your's has the fortune; Dibble's Mifs
Fairfax is the girl for your purpofe.

JACK.

But where is Dibble and his Mifs Fairfax? I have
danc'd attendance here a pretty while; what am I to
think of all this?

GREGORY.

What are you to think of it? why I'll tell you;
this young lady, d'ye fee—Now don't you go about,
Mafter Jacky, and fay that I told you, but this
young

young lady here, that you have been talking to, is—
Hark, fure your father's coming.

JACK.

I hear his foot upon the ftairs; my bones ake at
the found of it.

GREGORY.

Quick, quick, down the back ftairs, and away for
your life; fo, fo; that's well.   [*Exit Jack.*

Enter NIGHTSHADE.

NIGHTSHADE.

Why, Gregory, rafcal, hangdog! what's become
of you? run quickly down and drive thofe bawling
fellows from the gate.

GREGORY.

A herd of wolves as foon; they'll eat me up alive.
O lack-a-day, Sir, you know little of a London mob.

NIGHTSHADE.

Go down I tell you, Sirrah, and difperfe 'em.

GREGORY.

Why, Sir, 'tis more than my Lord Mayor can do:
There's a man knock'd o' the head they fay, and till
there's another or two to keep him company, they'll
never be at reft: Leave 'em to fight it out.

NIGHTSHADE.

Leave 'em! why blockhead, it is me they follow:
Nothing elfe fhould have driven me into this houfe
again.

GREGORY.

O Gemini, have you been knock'd o' the head?

NIGHTSHADE.

Why no, you fool, 'tis I have done the mifchief;
but the moft patient man alive cou'd do no lefs.

GREGORY.

Nay, Sir, if you have been playing the fame tune
upon their noddles, as you do upon mine, thefe
London fculls won't bear it; they are as brittle as a
Shrewfbury cake.

Enter

Enter STAPLETON.

STAPLETON.

Hey-day, friend Andrew, what is all this noise and outcry?

NIGHTSHADE.

I think the devil's in the people, you shall hear—As I was coming down the street, in meditation on the parson's pidgeon-house, a rascally scaramouch, in a short jerkin, with a cap and feather on his noddle, winds me a damn'd blast on his post horn, point-blank into my ear, flourishing his newspapers full in my face at the same time: Now as there are no two things I hate on earth like newspapers and noises, so I could not well avoid giving him a gentle remembrance with my cane upon his crown: The casket gave a cursed crack and down tumbled the politician: Instantly the raggamuffins collected, and I took refuge here in your court-yard.

STAPLETON.

Nay, if you have silenc'd the Morning Post, you had better have drag'd the speaker out of his coach, and beat his brains out with the mace. Do you consider how many enemies you make by stopping the circulation of abuse? 'tis as necessary to the city as the circulation of cash.

NIGHTSHADE.

Go down I tell you, fellow, and make up the matter with a dram; 'tis as much as any newspaper-head is worth in the kingdom; bid him not talk of damages; if my cane has split his scull, 'tis no more than his plaguy post-horn did by mine: He was the aggressor.

STAPLETON.

Hark'ee, you'll find the matter settled, but it will not be amiss to frighten him a little; you know how to manage it.   (*aside to Greg.*

GREGORY.

Most daintily I warrant you.   [*Exit.*

Enter

Enter Mrs. STAPLETON *and* LÆTITIA.

LÆTITIA.

O, Mr. Nightſhade, here's a piece of work!—this comes of being in a paſſion.

Mrs. STAPLETON.

A ſober citizen, a pains-taking induſtrious ſoul—

LÆTITIA.

A father of a family—eight helpleſs babes—I fear you've given him his laſt blow—Dear Sir, aſſiſt us!

(aſide.

NIGHTSHADE.

Laſt blow! what matters that, when he gave me the firſt!

Mrs. STAPLETON.

Well, well, heaven knows, but anger is a frightful thing; it turns a man into a fury. Defend me, I ſay, from a paſſionate man.

NIGHTSHADE.

And yet, madam, give me leave to tell you, you are enough to make one: Is it nothing to have our nerves lacerated, our whole fabrick ſhook to atoms by theſe horrid noiſes! The law ſhould provide againſt ſuch nuiſances.

STAPLETON.

The law regards breaking of heads as the greater nuiſance of the two—But here comes Gregory—Well, what has become of the poſtman?

Enter GREGORY.

GREGORY.

He has ſounded his laſt horn! You may ſleep in quiet for the future. I tender'd him the dram your honour was ſo good to offer; but his teeth are cloſed, he can't accept your favour.

Mrs. STAPLETON.

O horrible, you've kill'd the man!

STAPLETON.

What ſay the ſtanders-by on the occaſion?

GREGORY.

GREGORY.

They give him an extraordinary character; they say he deliver'd a hand bill and founded a posthorn better than any man in all the bills of mortality.

LÆTITIA

Thanks to Mr. Nightshade, he is likely to make a figure in the bills of mortality still—did you see the wound?

GREGORY.

A perilous gash, I'd not have such a star in my forehead to be the richest alderman in the city of London.

NIGHTSHADE.

'Tis a pity but he had been one, for then his horns might have warded off the blow.

GREGORY.

If I was your honour I would be looking out for the crowner; it will be well done to touch him pretty handsomely before he calls a quest upon the body.

Mrs. STAPLETON.

Has the gentleman thought of any witnesses?

GREGORY.

You must have a steady set to prevent accidents; unprejudic'd, impartial men, that were not present at the affair, these people will never do: For my part, if you think of subpænaying me, you are a lost man, if I was once to shew this head of mine in open court you wou'd be condemned upon the face of it.

NIGHTSHADE.

Hold your tongue, rascal, I don't believe a word you say: I'll go down and be satisfied with my own eyes.

STAPLETON.

Hold, hold, friend Andrew, I'll not suffer it; they'll tear you piecemeal: Stay where you are and let me see if I can't quiet 'em; they know me and will credit what I tell 'em: If it is as Gregory says I'll send him to the hospital; we'll save him, if it's possible.

NIGHT-

NIGHTSHADE.

Thank you, Mafter Stapleton, thank you heartily. That's friendly howfoever. .   *[Exit Stapleton.*

LÆTITIA. *(to Mrs. Stapleton.)*

Dear Madam, follow Mr. Stapleton, and perfuade him not to let him off; he muft be made to feel.

Mrs. STAPLETON.

I think he 'fhould, and will leave him in your hands.   *[Exit.*

LÆTITIA.

Ah, Mr. Nightfhade, will you never be brought off from this unhappy temper? You fee the difmal effects of it; you feel them; I perceive you do : Your compunction is fevere; I pity you—your fituation brings the tears into my eyes.

NIGHTSHADE.

It's more than it does into mine; I tell you it is all a collufion to extort money; and this rogue of mine falls in with the plot. Stapleton will tell another ftory.   •

LÆTITIA.

I am afraid not; prepare youfelf for the worft, and confider what attonement you can make to a difconfolate widow.

NIGHTSHADE.

Spare your pity, young madam, you don't yet know how eafy moft widows are to be comforted.

GREGORY.

To be fure, madam, his honour is in the right to bear up as they fay, but it will be a trapan at leaft : The china riviter at next door is a knowing man in fractures, and he fays his fcull will never ring well again fo long as it is a fcull. Oh, Sir, what will poor dear Mafter Jacky think of this? He's in the country, lord love him, and little dreams of this mifhap ; I fear 'twill break his heart.

NIGHTSHADE.

Hold your tongue, you blockhead. Well, Mr. Stapleton, you've feen the man.

K   *Re-enter*

Re-enter STAPLTON.

STAPLETON.

I've seen the man, and pacified the mob.

NIGHTSHADE.

That's well; and it all proves a false alarm?

STAPLETON.

I wish I cou'd say so—but we muft hope the beft.

NIGHTSHADE.

How! what! fure he is not in danger? This fellow's report I did not regard; your's alarms me.

STAPLETON.

Compofe yourfelf, however; the fymptoms, indeed, are unpromifing, but I have put him into good hands; he is convey'd to the London Hofpital. Be a man; I am forry to fee you fo uneafy.

LÆTITIA.

Dear Sir, 'tis natural; the worft of men have moments of compunction; it is not to be fuppofed that Mr. Nightfhade, though fatally addicted to paffion, is totally devoid of human feelings.

NIGHTSHADE.

I beg you'll be fo kind to leave me; I fhou'd wifh to have a minute's recollection. Gregory, you may ftay. *(He retires to the back fcene.*

STAPLETON.

Lætitia, I begin to pity him.

LÆTITIA.

Have patience: let him chew the cud of reflection. Remorfe, fometimes, like an advertifing quack, will make great commotion in a man's conftitution; but repentance is the regular phyfician, which by flow but fteady means, conducts the patient to his cure.

[*Exeunt Stapleton and Lætitia.*

NIGHTSHADE.

Gregory!

GREGORY.

Your honour! How fanctified he looks! as who fhou'd fay, Gregory, give me a good word on my trial.

NIGHTSHADE.

I'm thinking, Gregory, of this accident.

GRE-

GREGORY.

Well, Sir, and how do you like it?

NIGHTSHADE.

Why, I'm in hopes it will blow over; I think they'll hardly prosecute, and if the worst shou'd happen, they can make nothing of it, but chance-medley or manslaughter; nothing else, Gregory: So there's little to fear from the law. But as I am a man, who have always enforced the law against other people, d'ye observe me, and consequently made enemies amongst the wicked; I shou'd think, honest Gregory, you might stand in my place, and I'd be sure to bring you off, and reward you into the bargain.

GREGORY.

Lord, Sir, a trifle; I shou'd be proud of being hang'd in the service of so good a master; but I'm afraid there were too many people present, and 'twou'd be gross presumption to suppose any body cou'd mistake me for your honour.

NIGHTSHADE.

Why certainly that is a hard pill to swallow; but what is to be done?

GREGORY.

Make over your estate to Master Jacky, and fly your country: What if I run to the French walk, and take you a passage in the Boulogne Pacquet? I may be in time to secure the cabbin before any other malefactor has taken a birth in it.

NIGHTSHADE.

Malefactor! prythee let me hear no more of your advice, it is but wasting time; I must have better counsel; and tho' brother Manlove has not pleas'd me in the matter of the pigeon-house, yet he's a good man in the main, and understands his business; run to him, d'ye hear, and desire him to repair here directly, upon a pressing concern; I know he'll not refuse assistance when I really want him.

GREGORY.

I'll go directly—This is lucky.   (*aside.*

NIGHTSHADE.

And d'ye mind, leave me to open the affair to him; say nothing of the accident.

GREGORY.

No to be sure; a likely matter, truly.　　　[Exit.

NIGHTSHADE.

I wish I had not smote him quite so hard; and yet I shou'd have thought no mischief cou'd have follow'd; I've struck that clod-pate twice as hard, a hundred and a hundred times; 'tis that has spoilt my hand: it is surprising what some heads will bear; I wou'd I was with my poor boy in the country; what evil genius brought me up to this curst scene of mischief and mischance? Dear fortune, rescue me from this one scrape, and let me scramble out of the next as I can. [Exit.

Enter LÆTITIA followed by CHARLES.

LÆTITIA.

Now, Sir, be pleas'd to favour me with your commands.

CHARLES.

I am to solicit you in behalf of Mr. Manlove, that he may be allow'd the honour of making himself known to you.

LÆTITIA.

That is done already: I am no stranger to Mr. Manlove, believe me.

CHARLES.

So, so: she has discovered me—Well, Madam, if Mr. Manlove is already known to you in his assumed character, may he not hope to improve that acquaintance in his real one?

LÆTITIA.

The character he has assumed, I must fairly own to you, gives me no favourable opinion of his real one: The shallow devices he made use of to impose on my understanding, when he thought himself secure from a discovery, betray a disingenuous mind; and I must believe, that no man wou'd descend from the character of a gentleman, who was not wanting in the requisites that go to the support of it.

CHARLES.

CHARLES.

I've made myself a precious blockhead: This mummery of the painter has difgufted her. - *(afide.*

LÆTITIA.

As to his pretended tafte for painting, I will not affect more fkill than I poffefs, but I will venture to fay, that either he is ignorant of the art, or prefumes upon my being fo.

CHARLES.

I'm fairly trapp'd : I muft be prating of what I did not underftand—I will not offer much in Mr. Manlove's behalf, Madam; but as to his fkill in painting, you will be pleas'd to confider him not as a profeffor, but a lover only of the art.

LÆTITIA.

A lover, Sir! that is the laft character I fhou'd wifh to confider Mr. Manlove in.

CHARLES.

I perfectly underftand you, Mifs Fairfax : You have faid enough : Mr. Manlove underftands you : I believe I need not explain myfelf any farther.

LÆTITIA.

No, the cafe is perfectly clear; and I flatter myfelf you think I have been explicit on my part.

CHARLES.

There can be no complaint on that fcore. Nothing now remains for Mr. Manlove, but to lay afide, as foon as he is able, every thought, each hope that had Mifs Fairfax for its object.

LÆTITIA.

'Twill be much for my repofe.

CHARLES.

Rely upon it, then, your repofe fhall never be difturb'd by Mr. Manlove; never—Adieu. *(goes out.*

LÆTITIA.

Your fervant—He's piqued, and it becomes him.

CHARLES, *(returns.)*

If ever you fee him here again, fay I have deceiv'd you—let me bear the blame : Your moft obedient.

LÆTITIA.

Good day—I fhall depend upon you.

CHARLES.

CHARLES.

Set your mind at reft; I'll die before I break my word: Your fervant.   [*Exit.*

LÆTITIA. (*alone.*)

How wou'd this man plead in his own caufe! Ah, why wou'd fortune not concert with nature, and either give the wealth of Manlove to his merits; or purchafe out his merits to beftow on Manlove's wealth?

Enter LUCY *haftily.*

LUCY.

Where can this provoking cloak be laid? Every thing is in train, and there is not a moment to be loft—Ah!   (*fcreams.*

LÆTITIA.

Lucy! whither away fo faft?

LUCY.

I declare I did not fee you, Madam; I thought you was in your own room.

LÆTITIA.

But where are you running to, Child?

LUCY.

Only ftepping out a little way.

LÆTITIA.

Stepping out! whither?

LUCY.

To my brother Dibble's.

LÆTITIA,

For what?

LUCY.

Upon a little family bufinefs, that's all. I cou'd have fworn you had been with your gentleman in the painting-room.

LÆTITIA.

My gentleman! who is it you call my gentleman?

LUCY.

Humph—I'll fhow her that I am in her fecrets; it will keep her out of mine. (*afide.*) I thought you was with Mr. Manlove; I left you together.

LÆTITIA.

Mr. Manlove! what is this you tell me?

LUCY.

LUCY.

Nay, Madam, don't be alarm'd, I am no tell-tale; and though I knew Mr. Manlove in his painter's character, nobody shall be the wiser for me, I assure you.

LÆTITIA.

As sure as can be it is so! what a discovery! (*aside.*) Well, Lucy, I find you are in the secret; you know the real Mr. Manlove; but pray tell me who is the pretended one? I have been received at Mr. Manlove's house, and visited here, by a young man who calls himself Manlove: Who is he?

LUCY.

Oh, dear Ma'am. don't you know him?—I wish I don't get into a scrape, but there is no going back—(*aside.*) It is young Mr. Nightshade out of the country, Ma'am; he is come up incog, and is afraid his father shou'd discover him, that's all.

LÆTITIA.

Is that all? I shan't take your word for that. I suspect there is more in the plot than you have related. If this young man is afraid of being seen by his father, what brings him hither? Answer me that?

LUCY.

Madam, I—I—I can't tell what brings him hither.

LÆTITIA.

Lucy, don't equivocate; for I will know. I saw him leave the house just now with your brother, you are following in great haste; upon family business you pretend; but I suspect upon no fair errand: Confess to me, for you shall not stir to your brother's 'till you do.

LUCY.

As you will for that, Madam, but I cannot endure to be suspected, and I will confess to you when I have done crying. (*weeps.*

LÆTITIA.

Do so, you had best.

LUCY.

Why then you must know, that Mr. Manlove, that is, I mean Mr. Nightshade, that calls himself Mr. Manlove, is fallen monstrously in love with——

LÆTITIA.

With whom?   LUCY.

LUCY.

Me, Madam.—Vain creature! I know she thought it was herself   (*aside.*

LÆTITIA.

And you believ'd him, did you?

LUCY.

Yes, Madam, I believ'd him.

LÆTITIA.

Well, and what did he do then?

LUCY.

Nay nothing, Madam, that's all.

LÆTITIA.

Come, come, Lucy, but I know it is not all: You have given him your company, as you call it, have you not? and you are now going to meet him at your brother's, are you not?

LUCY.

No—yes—but if I am, it's all in fair and honest way of courtship: Oh, if he was to go for to offer any thing unhandsome to me, I should tear his eyes out. Nobody can say I have the least speck or flaw, no not so big as the point of a pin, on my reputation. It would be the death of me—I would sooner part from my life than my virtue; he has promis'd—

LÆTITIA.

What has he promis'd?

LUCY.

To marry me.

LÆTITIA.

Marry you! ridiculous.

LUCY.

Ay, I knew the jealous thing could not bear that; she will burst with envy.   (*aside.*

LÆTITIA.

Hark'ee, Lucy; I commend you for the honesty of your confession, run into my chamber; Mr. Stapleton is coming this way, and will interrupt us: Compose yourself, and we will talk over the affair at leisure. (*Exit Lucy.*) Happy, happy revolution! What a ridiculous mal-entendu had I fallen into! Oh how deliciously I will torture this fine gentleman-painter for his contrivances!   A.CT.

ACT V. SCENE I.

Enter JACK *and* DIBBLE.

DIBBLE.

COME along, Squire, the lady is expecting you at my apartment. Every thing is in train, and 'twill be your own fault now if you are not the happiest man in England.

JACK.

Hold a moment, Dibble, hold! My brother's coming and I can't refist the pleafure of a little natural exultation.

DIBBLE.

Perverfe, vexation! Are you mad?—By heavens you'll lofe the lady—and what is worfe, by heavens fhe'll loofe the gentleman!   (*afide.*

Enter CHARLES.

CHARLES.

So, Jack, I hope your frolick's at an end: you've been diforderly in your cups I find.

JACK.

Where did you hear that?

CHARLES.

Where I leaft wifh'd to hear it; at Mr. Stapleton's; Mifs Fairfax told me.

JACK.

Mifs Fairfax told you, did fhe fo? Mifs Fairfax was not very angry when fhe told you, I fhou'd guefs: You did not find me greatly out of favour, did you?

CHARLES.

In truth I had fo little occafion to boaft of my own reception, Jack, that I did not give much attention to what fhe faid of you.

L   JACK.

JACK.

That's honeſtly confeſſed however: So your reception was but cold, and you have drop'd all thoughts
of a connexion I ſuppoſe?

CHARLES.

Intirely: I've received my peremptory diſmiſſion.

JACK.

Poor Charles! you are diſmiſs'd? Your perſon,
genius, equipage, eſtate, all ſtand you in no ſtead?
Another is preferr'd before you—perhaps ſome
country booby like myſelf; and don't you wiſh you
knew the happy man?

CHARLES.

Not I.

DIBBLE.

What are you at? you'll ruin all.

JACK.

I ſhall burſt if I don't tell him—Brother, I believe
I cou'd direct you to the man that's done all the
miſchief.

CHARLES.

I give you credit, Jack, for that: I do believe
you've done me all the miſchief in your power.

JACK.

Who, I? Oh dear, you flatter me; a country
whelp ſupplant a travell'd gentleman like you? im-
poſſible—and yet——

CHARLES.

What yet?

JACK.

This witneſs on my finger here would ſtagger ſome
folks; I am apt to think Miſs Fairfax means to wear
it in good time.

CHARLES.

A wedding ring! you muſt excuſe me, Jack; I
want credulity for that.

JACK.

Juſt as you pleaſe; I bought it for her wearing,
and meaſur'd her finger for that purpoſe, and did intend with the parſon's help to put it on with that
deſign,

DIBBLE.

DIBBLE.

Will nothing ſtop your mouth? By heavens I'll throw the matter up,   (*aſide to Jack.*

CHARLES.

You! you marry Miſs Lætitia Fairfax!

DIBBLE.

Dear 'Squire be perſuaded, and come away.
(*aſide to Jack.*

JACK.

Hold your tongue I tell you—I, I, and not the ingenious, learned, travell'd Mr. Manlove; here's a witneſs that will vouch for what I ſay. (*Dibble offers to go.*) Where are you running?—come back. Tell my brother what you know of Miſs Fairfax's partiality for a certain, inſignificant, ignorant fellow, call'd Jack Nightſhade.

DIBBLE.

For ſhame, Sir, you ſhould not talk of lady's favours.

CHARLES.

Your friend is cautious you perceive.

JACK.

Hang him, he's ſo by habit; he's a lawyer—but ſpeak out: You are come to fetch me to Miſs Fairfax, and Miſs Fairfax is at your lodgings, and I am to be the lady's huſband, and the bill is a true bill, is it not?

DIBBLE.

It is.

CHARLES.

Errors excepted—You forgot your caution. This can never be. Hark'ee, Sir; a little croſs examination if you pleaſe.

JACK.

As much of that as you think proper. He's us'd to that ſport; he'll dodge like a rabbit in a warren.

CHARLES.

You ſay the lady is at your lodgings: Anſwer me, what lady?

DIBBLE.

DIBBLE.

Sir, I believe—what lady?—that's your queſtion—what lady is at my lodgings?

CHARLES.

Ay, Sir, without equivocation,

DIBBLE.

Well, Sir, I am not upon oath in this buſineſs; nor am I obliged to aſcertain the identity of people's perſons; but the lady at my lodgings I take to be Miſs Fairfax.

JACK.

Does that ſatisfy you? Brother, I thank you for your coat; it has made an impreſſion you perceive.

CHARLES.

Have a little patience—You take her to be Miſs Fairfax?—deſcribe her perſon.

DIBBLE.

I never meddled with her perſon, Sir; that's not for me to do.

CHARLES.

Is ſhe fair complexion'd?

DIBBLE.

I think ſo.

JACK.

I can't ſay I do.

CHARLES.

Light hair, or dark?

DIBBLE.

My eyes are none of the beſt, but I think Miſs Fairfax's hair is white.

JACK.

Black as a crow, by Jupiter.

CHARLES.

Tall, or ſhort?

DIBBLE.

I never meaſur'd her but, I take her to be tall.

JACK.

Death and the devil, why you're drunk! Fair, tall, light-hair'd! why ſhe's a little, dapper, duſky damſel, with a poll as black as——

CHARLES.

Hark'ee, Sir, a word in your ear. *(to Dibble.*

DIBBLE.

DIBBLE.

Blown, as I hope to be a judge ! *(aside.*

CHARLES.

You have a sister answers this description : You're discover'd and a villain. *(aside to Dibble.*

JACK.

Hold, hold, no closeting of witnesses.

DIBBLE.

Good Sir, be not offended. Mr. Nightshade first borrow'd your name, and my sister to keep up the jest, made free with that of Miss Fairfax—nothing but a frolick.

CHARLES.

What do you tell me ? did my brother take my name in any interview with Miss Fairfax ?

DIBBLE.

Certainly, Sir ; she calls him Mr. Manlove at this moment.

CHARLES.

Away ; your news has saved your ears, away.

DIBBLE.

'Egad we are all blown up : I must go and tell Lucy to make her peace. [*Exit.*

JACK.

How now ; what's this ? Hollo ! where's Dibble running ?

CHARLES.

Your humble Servant, Mr. Manlove—Take my name, my credit from me, Jack ? It is too much. You must be saved however.

JACK.

I must be satisfied. Is this fair dealing ? Where is Dibble gone ?

CHARLES.

Let him go where he will ; he has made a fool of you.

JACK.

Yes, but I'm not a fool to take your word for that ; so let me pass.

CHARLES.

Nay, Jack, but hear reason——

JACK.

JACK.

Yes, and while you are reasoning, I shall lose the lady.

CHARLES.

I say the lady; have a care she does not prove the lady's maid.

JACK.

The maid! ah, brother, I'm too cunning to take that upon trust. You have raised my curiosity however, and I will know the truth----So let me go, for go I will, and that's enough. [*Exit.*

CHARLES.

A match, we'll start together. My happiness is sure as much concern'd in this discovery, as your's.

(*follows him.*

SCENE II. *Stapleton's House.*

Enter NIGHTSHADE *and* MANLOVE.

NIGHTSHADE.

I should think, brother, there's no danger but a jury will see the action in this light.

MANLOVE.

'Tis hard to say; juries are ticklish things; the law will look to the motives: *If it shall appear that it was done not from the wickedness of the heart, but from the sudden heat of the passions,* a jury will bring it in *Manslaughter.*

NIGHTSHADE.

Well, and don't all the world know there's not a more passionate man living than myself?

MANLOVE.

You have sometimes told me I was passionate; I never heard you say as much for yourself.

NIGHTSHADE.

But if there was no malice in the deed, how can it ever be deem'd murder?

MANLOVE.

Malice is threefold: First, malice express; secondly, malice implied; thirdly, malice prepense: Of each in their order——

NIGHT-

NIGHTSHADE.
Pſhaw! pr'ythee, what avails defcribing any, when I've none of all the three?

MANLOVE.
Had you no quarrel then before the act?

NIGHTSHADE.
Quarrel! why no----or if I had, 'twas only a few words.

MANLOVE.
Is that the cane you ſtruck him with?

NIGHTSHADE.
This is the twig; I call it nothing more.

MANLOVE.
I doubt the law will conſtrue it a weapon of offence.

NIGHTSHADE.
And pray now was not his a weapon of offence? I believe the whole town thinks it ſuch, of great offence; ſick or well, there's no repoſe for thoſe horns. What I did was in ſelf-defence.

MANLOVE.
I fear 'twill not be thought ſo: If indeed you had any *wound to ſhew whereby the violence of the battery might be proved*——

NIGHTSHADE.
Wound! why I have a wound as bad an one as his; only mine lies within ſide of my head, and his without: He has broke the drum of my ears.

MANLOVE.
What do you talk of ears? if you had been happy enough now to have *loſt a finger, an eye, or a foretooth, it would have been the loſs of a defenſive member, and a mayhem at common law.*

NIGHTSHADE.
Well, brother, be ſo kind to tell me what I am to do.

MANLOVE.
Repent.

NIGHTSHADE.

Why fo I will, provided you fay nothing about the matter, and my country acquits me upon trial; but if I am to be punifhed for my faults, what fignifies repenting of 'em into the bargain?

MANLOVE.

Well, Andrew, I muft tell you 'there is yet a way of getting honourably out of this affair, provided you will bind yourfelf to me, never to lift your hand in wrath againft a fellow creature.

NIGHTSHADE.

Why no, to be fure I fhan't; I thought all fculls were as hard as Gregory's.

MANLOVE.

Come; you muft have done with Gregory's; nay, I wou'd not alone exempt man from your fury, but beaft likewife: Cruelty muft not be practifed in any fhape: Nature muft not be wounded in any of her works.   Promife me this upon the faith of an honeft man, and I'll redeem you from this fcrape.

NIGHTSHADE.

Look'ee, Brother, I am fenfible of the folly of it, but as it's impoffible to fay where temptation may lead, there lies the fatal weapon; ufe it who will; I'll never take another ftick in hand, till I'm obliged to go upon crutches.   *(throws down his cane.*

MANLOVE.

Say you fo, then I'll cure your broken head in an inftant.   Come with me, and you fhall fee what difpatch I can make upon occafion.   [*Exeunt.*

SCENE III. *The Painting Room.*

LÆTITIA *is difcover'd painting*; LUCY *attending*; *a layman placed at fome diftance.*

LÆTITIA.

Thefe touches come off well; this laft fitting was a good one: Methinks I never was in better look. Lucy, what fay you? is it like?

LUCY.

LUCY.

Like, Madam! 'tis alive; 'tis Mr. Stapleton himself.

LÆTITIA.

Is the servant gone for his cloaths to dress the layman? I'll positively rub in the drapery now I'm about it. Well, child, I've turn'd this matter in my head, and I believe I must forgive you; there's no holding out against contrition; I believe your brother was to blame—so this painter then is Mr. Manlove?

LUCY.

Yes, madam, and a lovely man he is; if you please to remember, I told you so the first moment I saw him; so genteel, so well-bred, so perfectly the gentleman. Oh, here comes Thomas with the cloaths—shall I help to put 'em on?

Enter SERVANT.

LÆTITIA.

So, so! that's right—let the arm fall naturally— it's very well as it is—Now turn the layman with its side to me—no, t'other way—a little more. Stay, let me do it myself. Now stand away—that's it.

SERVANT.

Have you any further commands, madam?

LÆTITIA.

No; yes. If the young gentleman who was with me this morning should call again, shew him up hither.

SERVANT.

The painter?

LÆTITIA.

Yes, the painter, as you call him.

SERVANT.

Madam, he is this moment come into the courtyard.

LÆTITIA.

Indeed! then do as I bid you. (*Exit Ser.*) So, so, he has found out the mistake as well as myself.

M   LUCY.

LUCY.

Pray, Madam, give me leave to go and shew Mr.
Manlove hither.

LÆTITIA.

Do so, Lucy, do so—What a flutter am I in!—but,
hark'ee, don't give him any intimation that I know
him. (*Exit Lucy.*) This is happy! I am such a gainer
by this revolution that I cannot find in my heart to
be angry with the girl—That ever I shou'd be the
bubble of so gross an imposition! Hark; he's coming.
I'll pretend to be at work! tho' I am so confused
I don't know one colour from another. O heavens,
how charmingly he looks!   (*she rises.*

Enter CHARLES.

CHARLES.

I ask a thousand pardons; I entreat I mayn't dis-
turb you.

LÆTITIA.

Oh, Sir, don't mention it: You see I use no ceremony.

CHARLES.

You're infinitely obliging. I have ventur'd once
again, Miss Fairfax, to intrude upon your patience.

LÆTITIA.

As often as you please; you're always welcome
here. Come hither—I must have your judgement.
How do you like what I have done?

CHARLES.

All that you do is well; but you'll forgive me, I
am full of other thoughts, and wish to lose no moment of this happy opportunity.

LÆTITIA.

Pish! I must have you flatter me: Sit down—
This drappery puzzles me—Sit down, I say: Your
modern habits are so stiff. How shall I manage it?
Come, take the chalk; nay, no excuse: Though you
are so smartly drest, you absolutely must assist me.

CHARLES.

I beg to be excus'd: my happiness is staked upon
this crisis; my heart is full and must have vent.

LÆTITIA.

L Æ T I T I A.

How can you be fo tirefome ? Now you are going upon the old topick, Mr. Manlove.

CHARLES.

I muft confefs it is of him that I wou'd fpeak.

L Æ T I T I A.

Fye, fye upon you! call to mind your promife. Hold—fuppofe I throw afide this ugly brown and gold, and put him in a fancy drefs; What fay you ?

CHARLES.

Nothing ; for I am nothing : I have no art, no faculty of painting ; I am an impoftor. On my knees I do befeech you, forgive and hear me.

L Æ T I T I A.

Pray be compofed, nor let your zeal for Mr. Manlove agitate you thus. I'll fave you all this trouble, by confeffing freely to you, I have chang'd my mind fince laft we parted.

CHARLES.

Chang'd ! as how ?

L Æ T I T I A.

As you'll be pleas'd to hear. I think of Mr. Manlove now as favourably as you yourfelf cou'd wifh.

CHARLES.

Madam——

L Æ T I T I A.

I think the woman muft be bleft, whom fuch a man fhall honour with his choice.

CHARLES.

Indeed ! I may prefume then you wou'd condefcend to countenance his addreffes.

L Æ T I T I A.

That's a home queftion ; but I think it is not eafy to deny him any thing.

CHARLES.

I'm thunderftruck ! The boy has told me the truth, fhe likes him and I am undone.

L Æ T I T I A.

What is the matter now ? You feem quite difconcerted. Is not this the very point you aim'd at ? Hav'n't I confeft all that you wifh'd ?

CHARLES.

CHARLES.

Oh, no! You torture me.

LÆTITIA.

Man, reftlefs man! whom nothing I can do will fatisfy: Offended when I refufe your friend; when I accept him, tortur'd.

CHARLES.

And tortur'd I muft be: for know, moft wretched as I am, it is not for a friend I plead, but for myfelf.

LÆTITIA.

Well, Sir, I'm free to fay, I ftill abide by my confeffion: What you tell me fhakes not my efteem for Mr. Manlove.

CHARLES.

Then I have loft you; for that Manlove is my younger brother, and has won you under a fictitious name: I that really own it, am difcarded.

LÆTITIA.

How purblind you long-fighted wits fometimes can be! You tell me you are Mr. Manlove; have I revok'd my opinion? You fay your brother took your name; have I exprefs'd myfelf in favour of Mr. Nightfhade?

CHARLES.

O heavens! I do begin to hope——

LÆTITIA.

You fhou'd not puzzle me with fuch crofs purpofes. Will you be Mr. Manlove, and believe what I now fay of him, or give that name to your brother, and hear me repeat what I lately faid of him?

CHARLES.

Oh, let me be what you approve; I afk no higher bleffing.

LÆTITIA.

We are interrupted. See, your formidable rival! Oh, you have made a fine confufion—Come away.

[Exeunt.

Enter JACK.

JACK.

Hift! hark'ee! brother Charles!—He won't turn back, and I dare not follow him, for fear I run into old

old Crufty's jaws: I am fain to go as warily in this
houfe as if I was riding over a warren. Didlikins!
here comes the girl at laft—Oh, fye upon you, Mifs,
oh fye—

Enter L U C Y *haftily.*

L U C Y.

Hufh! hufh! A truce to your reproaches—Hide
yourfelf; your father's at my heels.

J A C K.

My father! Drown it! what fhall I do now?

L U C Y.

Here, get behind this layman; ftoop: ftand clofe:
I'll put the fhutters to; I owe you that good turn, at
leaft, to bring you off.   Stand clofe!

Enter N I G H T S H A D E.

N I G H T S H A D E.

So, fo! What's doing here? Darknefs at mid-day!
Your fervant, Mr. Stapleton; I fee you notwithftand-
ing; there you are: Fine goings on at your age:
Smuggling your chambermaids in corners—Call you
this fair trading? Oh, if your wife faw this.

J A C K. *(from behind.)*

For pity's fake keep him off.   He's coming!

L U C Y.

Where are you coming, Sir? Pray leave the room;
your company difturbs him; don't you fee how ill he is?

N I G H T S H A D E.

Poor gentleman! and fo you fhut out the light to
make him better? Ay, let him lean upon you, com-
fort him; I dare be fworn he has need of it—Shame
upon you, Mafter Stapleton! What you'll not fpeak,
not you.   Here comes one will make you fpeak, and
ftir too, to fome tune.   Here, Madam, here's your
virtuous hufband; here's a picture of modern con-
jugal fidelity.

Enter

Enter · Mrs. STAPLETON.

Mrs. STAPLETON.

A picture truly, for I think you're talking to nothing elfe : Why don't the girl open the fhutters? What do you ftand there for? O, ho !   *(fees Jack.*

Enter STAPLETON *and* MANLOVE.

STAPLETON.

What my old friend, conferring with the layman ! Break his head, Andrew, if you pleafe ; no man-flaughter can lie there.   *(the window is opened.*

NIGHTSHADE.

How's this ! why I proteft I took it for yourfelf; and I was fcandaliz'd to fee a fober citizen in fuch clofe conference with a damfel of fo great temptations.

MANLOVE.

Come, brother, you have had one warning againft anger, let this be a memento to guard againft fufpicion.

NIGHTSHADE.

Brother, you know I can't endure advice ; I fee my error ; that's enough.

Mrs. STAPLETON.

Yes, but you don't fee all ; there's more behind the fcenes ; your greateft error, Mr. Nightfhade, is not yet found out.

NIGHTSHADE.

Why, what the vengeance have we here ? Come out : Let's fee your face. Son Jack ! Furies and flames! My boy as I'm alive.

MANLOVE.

This is judgement upon judgement.

NIGHTSHADE.

Which of you all have conjur'd up this plot ? Oh, thou unutterably vile and forry puppy ! Hound, that I have bred to tear my heart out—Jack, Jack, Jack, for you to ufe me thus ; you whom I've made my boaft, the ftaff of my old age—I wou'd I had a ftaff, I'd beat your brains out with it, blockhead, fo I wou'd.

MANLOVE.

Hold, hold, no more of that ; remember promifes.

NIGHT-

NIGHTSHADE.

And in that jacket too; the fubftance of a farm
laid out upon your back: Sirrah, whence came that
conjuror's coat, that fcoundrel's livery? Anfwer me.

JACK

Father, 'tis none of mine; 'tis brother Charles's.

NIGHTSHADE.

There, Mr. Manlove! there's your pretty gentleman! a fine account; the corrupter of his brother.

STAPLETON.

Be more patient, friend Andrew.

NIGHTSHADE.

I won't be patient; I've a father's privilege to juf-
tify my paffion. Hark'ee, Sir, what brought you
up to town? Who feduced you hither? I fuppofe
the fafhionable fcoundrel who lent you that fool's coat.

JACK.

Lord love you, father, 'twas a frolic of my own:
Charles wou'd have had me travell'd home again.

MANLOVE.

Was that like a feducer?

JACK.

And fo I fhou'd afore now, but that I fell into a
kind of a love-fuit here, with the young lady of this
houfe.

Mrs. STAPLETON.

What do you fay? a love-fuit!

STAPLETON.

With my ward, Mifs Fairfax? impoffible.

LUCY.

Ay, now comes my examination: I had beft efcape.
                                                (afide.

JACK.

Hold, hold; my whole defence turns upon your
teftimony—Stay where you are.   (To Lucy.

NIGHTSHADE.

Ay, let us hear; there's fomething in this plea:
Let us hear more of the love-fuit.

JACK.

Nay, 'twas not much of a fuit neither; it was very
foon over; Mifs was coming, Dibble got a licence,
and I bought a ring.   STA-

STAPLETON.

Why you're befide yourfelf, young man.

NIGHTSHADE.

Go on! the boy fpeaks well, and fhan't be brow-beat: Hear him out.

JACK.

And fo, as I was telling you, I fhou'd have married her out-right, if brother Charles had not thrown a fpoke in my wheel.

NIGHTSHADE.

See there, fee there! What fay you for your favorite now? Prove what you fay, my lad, and I will do-you juftice to the extent of my eftate.

JACK.

Say you fo, father? then it fhall out: Why brother Charles, you muft know, had a month's mind for the lady himfelf; fo he pretended to perfuade me that I was made a fool of, and that the girl I was going to marry was not Mifs Fairfax.

NIGHTSHADE.

There, there! you hear it now from the tongue of truth and innocence: You're fatisfied, I hope. I beg the lady may be fent for in.

JACK.

Sent for! a pretty joke; why there fhe ftands.

Mr. and Mrs. STAPLETON,

Ha. ha, ha!

NIGHTSHADE.

I'm thunderftruck.

JACK.

And fo am I; for if it had not been for brother Charles, as fure as you are here alive, we had both been happy before now.

NIGHTSHADE,

This, this the lady?

JACK.

Ay, father, that's fhe: I hope you like her.

STAPLETON.

Lucy! Lucy Dibble!

MANLOVE,

The fifter of my clerk!

NIGHT.

NIGHTSHADE.

Death and the devil! a chambermaid!

Mrs. STAPLETON.

Oh, you infidious huffy! what can you fay for yourfelf?

LUCY.

I am not here upon my trial, madam; that is paft, and Mifs Fairfax has fign'd my pardon. As for this gentleman, if I did put a little trick upon him under my miftrefs's name, he paid me in my own coin, by pafling himfelf off under his brother's. The parties reprefented are not prefent; but let me ftand at Mifs Fairfax's fide, and place him by Mr. Manlove, and I leave the world to decide which is the greateft impoftor of the two.

JACK.

Oh, you abominable little vixen!

MANLOVE.

Keep your peace, Jack, wou'd you prove your valour on a woman?

JACK.

Then by Jupiter, I'll break every bone in lawyer Dibble's fkin, before this day's at an end.

STAPLETON.

Underftand yourfelf, child; the daughter of a footman is no mate for the fon of a gentleman.

NIGHTSHADE.

To be fure: Well faid, Mafter Stapleton!

LUCY.

True, Sir, but the footman bred his daughter as a gentleman fhou'd, and the gentleman gave his fon the education of a footman. [*Exit.*

MANLOVE.

Brother Andrew——

NIGHTSHADE.

Pooh!

JACK.

Father, that laft wipe was at you.

NIGHTSHADE.

Hold your tongue, blockhead; get you home into the country, till the foil, and be a beaft of burden; 'tis what nature meant you for.

N

MAN-

MANLOVE.

Nay, brother, blame not nature, fhe has done her part: 'Tis you that fhou'd have till'd the foil. O Charles, you come upon a wifh; your father is impatient to embrace you.

Enter CHARLES.

CHARLES.

Let but my father add his approbation, and my happinefs fhall be compleat.

MANLOVE.

He can't withhold it. Come, throw prejudice afide; let wrath and jealoufy be caft far from you: Look upon this youth; he is your fon; you are the principle, but do you fubftitute the juftice to confefs my fyftem has fucceeded; it is poffible you fee to gain a knowledge of this world, and not be tainted with its wickednefs.

NIGHTSHADE.

'Tis mighty well; but for this cub of mine I'll difinherit him to the devil; I cou'd find in my heart, to die to-morrow, for the pleafure of cutting him off with a fhilling.

JACK.

Lord, father, in that cafe a little matter wou'd content me.

MANLOVE.

Come, come, the law has made provifion againft that: Jack muft inherit your eftate die when you will.

NIGHTSHADE.

Then I'll not die at all; I'll live for ever on purpofe to plague him; I'll ftarve the whelp; he fhall have nothing to live upon, but rain-water and pig-nuts.

MANLOVE.

Then, Andrew, I will keep him; he fhall live with me.

NIGHTSHADE.

Say you fo, brother? then I'll forgive him and keep him to myfelf; and fince you talk of knowledge of the world, I'll fhew him what it is: Come hither,

Jack,

Jack: I'll go with him as far as there is water to carry
us; I'll travel him to the world's end: Zounds, I'll
take him out of it, rather than be out-gone.

JACK.

Take the laſt ſtage by yourſelf, dear father.
Farewel, uncle; good-bye, Charles!

[Exeunt Nightſhade and Jack.

MANLOVE.

Incorrigible humouriſt! Come my ſon, and come
my worthy friends: Where is your amiable ward?
I ſtill have hopes this day of rancour and confuſion
will conclude with joy.

STAPLETON.

And ſo it ſhall, if my perſuaſion can have weight.

Mrs. STAPLETON.

Perſuaſion never fails, when inclination aids it.
Look, ſhe comes.

CHARLES.

And comes like hope, like ſpring and ſunſhine to
the longing year, with ſmiles of ſoft complacency
and love.

Enter LÆTITIA.

LÆTITIA.

Ay, now your rival's gone, you think the field
your own; but every hour will raiſe freſh rivals, for
every hour will draw forth freſh perfeſtions from a
character like your's, and each demand the preference
in our admiration and applauſe.

STAPLETON.

Well ſaid, my girl, then there's a bargain made:
What need of further words?

Mrs. STAPLETON.

Fye upon you, Mr. Stapleton, you diſtreſs her;
you are too much in haſte about theſe matters..

Mrs. STAPLETON.

Why, Dolly, you and I concluded our matter
within the week.

Mrs. STAPLETON.

Longer, 'twas longer: Don't believe him, Lætitia.

LÆTITIA.

LÆTITIA.

Excufe me, I can readily believe that hearts fo fitted for each other might unite at once by mutual attraction.

MANLOVE.

Doſt thou believe it, fair one? then away with all delay! not even the law, its own parent, ſhall be privileg'd in this caſe; we'll work like ſhipwrights at an armament, and Dibble, as a puniſhment for his intrigues, ſhall labour double tides. If marriage ever ſhall regain its dignity in this degenerate age, it muſt be by the union of ſuch hearts as theſe.

F I N I S.

www.ingramcontent.com/pod-product-compliance
Lightning Source LLC
Chambersburg PA
CBHW020804020726
47495CB00008B/2589